"You bid two hundred dollars."

"I had competition," Preston replied.

"Ah." Lulu narrowed her eyes. "So you're competitive?"

Preston shrugged. "No more than the next guy."

"But you wanted to win badly enough to—"

He tugged the donut box back from her lap. "I had my reasons."

Of course—the donuts. That made more sense. Lulu was a good cook…she knew her donuts were legendary around town. So why did that fact feel more discouraging than complimentary?

"Okay, your turn. You said you came to ask me something."

"I did." His gaze grew serious as it lingered back on hers. "It's a little wacky. I guess that's why I've been stalling."

He was going to ask her out. Her heart pounded hard beneath her dress. What else could it be? Why else would he have sat here this long with her? All the signs clearly pointed to him wanting to take her on a *real*—

"I need you to pretend to be my girlfriend for Christmas dinner."

Betsy St. Amant is the author of over twenty romance novels and novellas. She resides in North Louisiana with her hubby, two daughters, an impressive stash of coffee mugs and one furry schnauzer-toddler. Betsy has a BA in communications and a deep-rooted passion for seeing women restored to truth. When she's not composing her next book or trying to prove unicorns are real, Betsy can be found somewhere in the vicinity of an iced coffee. She writes frequently for www.ibelieve.com, a devotional site for women.

Books by Betsy St. Amant

Love Inspired

Visit the Author Profile page at LoveInspired.com for more titles.

Their Holiday Secret
Betsy St. Amant

LOVE INSPIRED
INSPIRATIONAL ROMANCE

LOVE INSPIRED®
INSPIRATIONAL ROMANCE

Recycling programs
for this product may
not exist in your area.

ISBN-13: 978-1-335-59843-1

Their Holiday Secret

Copyright © 2023 by Betsy St. Amant

For questions and comments about the quality of this book, please contact us
at CustomerService@Harlequin.com.

Love Inspired
22 Adelaide St. West, 41st Floor
Toronto, Ontario M5H 4E3, Canada
www.LoveInspired.com

Printed in U.S.A.

Wherefore putting away lying,
speak every man truth with his neighbour:
for we are members one of another.
—*Ephesians* 4:25

To my mama—thanks for taking me to my first writer's conference. Look what you started!

Acknowledgments

Where would a girl be without her Super Agent? Tamela Hancock Murray, I hope you don't tire of me thanking you in every book because I don't plan to stop! And as always, I appreciate Emily Rodmell and the entire editorial team at Love Inspired for making my books shine. Also special thanks to Georgiana Daniels and Megan Schaulis for being fabulous crit partners and encouraging me during this tight deadline.

To the amazing young adults at my church who eagerly consume the donuts we bring every week to Sunday School—love you guys! You provide the best character inspiration. Thanks for being so "slay" and teaching me the current lingo…and not laughing when I use it! You are the Claudia, Tori, Aiden and Haylee to my Lulu. Hugs!

To my readers—you guys are the best. Without you, my books couldn't exist. Thanks for the encouraging emails, newsletter subscriptions, positive reviews and marketing you do for my novels. It's all appreciated!

Big hugs to my family for supporting me with each new book and deadline. And to my Heavenly Father, for giving me ample opportunity to write stories. May they only ever bring Him glory! Soli Deo gloria.

Chapter One

Friday

Lulu Boyd knew donuts. She knew exactly which flavors worked best with cream fillings, which glazes needed sprinkles and the exact temperature the oil should be to achieve the ideal crispness of the dough. She even knew how to pipe icing into the shape of mistletoe and how to sugar-dust donut holes for extra crunch.

What she *didn't* know, however, was how to not make a fool of herself in front of the handsome new high school teacher who came in at 7:10 a.m. every Friday morning to purchase said donut holes.

The bell on the door chimed and Lulu turned, her eye on the daisy clock mounted on the wall, smiling casually as if her heart wasn't leaping into her throat. She swiped her hands down the front of her Oopsy Daisy Donuts apron—the one she designed herself with the flower logo—as a wave of disappointment washed over her.

Not him.

"Good morning, Sandy." She donned a fresh pair of gloves and began boxing up the spin instructor's regular order as a rush of cold December air followed her inside. Now that it was nearing the holidays, the older blonde always went for the chocolate donuts with the peppermint shavings. "You're going to have your class working hard for these, aren't you?"

"I find they pedal faster when there's a reward at the end." Sandy grinned, tucking her fitted hoodie down over the top of her yoga pants. "You should come try a class. We could even barter." She tapped the top of the donut box on the counter.

"Maybe after the holidays." Lulu said that last year, too. But this time, maybe she'd actually keep a New Year's resolution. This year's tentative resolution to start dating again had flopped—and she'd spent eleven months convincing herself to try. But after her ex-fiancé, Neal, had scooped up her heart a few years ago and proceeded to toss it on the ground at the first sign of his parents' disapproval, well…easier said than done. A spin class would probably be a lot less painful than a blind date. They always seemed to inevitably lead to the same place—nowhere.

The door chimed again, and this time Lulu didn't have to look to know.

It was *him*. Standing right under the mistletoe some of the mischievous high schoolers had hung there just last week.

Nope. Definitely not dating. Maybe next year.

Lulu spun toward her customer. Spin class it was. "You know what?" She snagged the debit card Sandy slid toward the cash register and swiped it. "I might just take you up on that."

"Sounds great." Sandy tucked her card into her purse and turned with her box of donuts, narrowly missing the broad chest draped in a tapered winter coat walking up behind her. "Oops, excuse me. Or should I say *oopsy daisy*?" She winked at Lulu before ducking out of the shop.

And then there were two.

Lulu finally lifted her gaze from his jacket to meet Preston Green's eyes.

"Good morning." His rich baritone filled the small space, and Lulu's pulse skittered. Just because she'd sworn off dating—or trusting—handsome men didn't mean she was blind to them and their effects.

She tugged off her gloves and tossed them into the waste bin behind the counter, having no doubt how well his deep voice commanded his classroom.

"Good morning." She fought the urge to sing-song Preston's name at the end like a class greeting their teacher. She chuckled at the sudden thought, and his eyes filled with amusement.

"What's so funny?" He leaned against the counter, one hand casually shoved into his coat pocket as he gave her his full attention. As if he wasn't on his way to work and had all the time in the universe.

Except she couldn't admit what she'd been thinking. Talk about awkward. She moved toward the donut hole tray, dismissively waving a pair of mini tongs and wishing she could dismiss how attractive he looked with that stubborn hint of scruff rising above the top of a hunter green scarf. "Oh, just... I heard a joke earlier, that's all." Lame excuse, but it was all she had.

"I love a good pun." Preston shifted his weight, the friendly glint never leaving his eyes. "Maybe I can tell it to my students. They're still warming up to me, honestly."

"Still?"

"I've been teaching here a little over three months now, but..." His voice trailed off and he shrugged. "I guess you could say some have come around faster than others."

Lulu frowned, her hand stilling on the tongs.

The students who frequented Oopsy Daisy after school several times a week thought highly of their new teacher from what she'd heard, but maybe they didn't let on in front of him. She didn't want to say anything prematurely, but she hated the thought of him feeling inaccurately judged.

She knew a little too much about that to let it happen to someone else.

"You're wrong," she blurted out. Then she pressed her lips together. That hadn't been as subtle as she'd intended. Which is what typically happened—every time she felt caught off guard or uncomfortable, she lost her filter.

"What do you mean?" Confusion simmered in his blue gaze.

She pointed with her tongs. "They *do* like you. I hear things around here." Now it was her turn to shrug. "When you feed teenagers sugar, they tend to talk."

"Is that right?" The amusement returned to his eyes. "I suppose I've been placing my donut holes in the wrong room each Friday, then. Apparently, my students need them more than my colleagues."

"Hey, you could always double your order." She clicked the tongs in his direction, trying to be cute, then grimaced. What was she doing? She looked like a crab clacking its claws. A rush of heat crept up her neck and under her short, dark, wavy bob.

"So—the joke?" he prompted. "I might not be able to feed them, but I can hopefully make them laugh."

"Right." Lulu cleared her throat. "Um…" A joke. No pressure. She swallowed hard as she snatched donut holes from the tray and dropped them into an Oopsy Daisy logo sack, her mind racing to come up with something. "Why did the donut go to the dentist?"

Preston crossed his arms over his chest, his jacket pulled taut across his shoulders. His brown hair, always perfectly gelled into place, didn't budge as he leaned in a little closer. Once again, he looked as if he had all the time in the world *and* really wanted to know. "Why?"

"It needed a filling," Lulu muttered as she mentally face-palmed herself.

He snorted, then grinned. "That's pretty good."

Was it? She folded the top of the sack of donut holes and felt her courage flare. Not bad for on the fly. In that case… "How busy was the donut's day?"

He raised a dark eyebrow, folding both arms against the countertop. "I can't imagine."

"It was jam-packed."

His head dropped forward, his shoulders shaking under his coat. "I don't know if that was better or worse."

"Your laugh was bigger, if that helps you determine." She slid his order toward him. "Here you go. Maybe split the spoils this time—half in homeroom, half in the teachers' lounge?"

"I like the way you think."

"I threw in a few extra." Oops. She hadn't meant to say that, either. She didn't want him thinking she was fishing for a thank-you or a tip. It was times like these she thought maybe Neal's parents had a point. She wasn't very couth. Thanks to her father's abandonment, she'd grown up in a low-income neighborhood that was probably the exact opposite of the word.

Though that was also the reason why she donated a lot of her time to the Haven Project—especially now, with the nonprofit's annual Home for the Holidays giveaway in the works. Swinging a hammer and keeping the construction crew full of donated coffee and donuts was the least she could do to help meet a community need. Neal had never understood that. He gave to charities, but his efforts were through signing a check—never getting his hands dirty.

Lulu squinted at Preston. He seemed a lot like Neal on the surface. Handsome, intelligent, charming with good manners—except he was much nicer.

But then again, hadn't Neal been nice at first, too? And hadn't her father been a friendly guy?

See. *This* was why she was going to spin class. Much safer than trying to force herself back into the dating world prematurely.

"I sincerely appreciate both the bonus donuts and the comedy." Preston dipped his head at her as he began backing toward the door, and she tried not to notice the way his gaze lingered on hers—like she actually had something to offer. "I better run. See you next Friday."

"I'll be here." She watched as he held the door open for the elderly Mr. Draper as he clamored inside with his cane, then lifted one hand in a wave as he strolled up the sidewalk toward Tulip Mound High.

She'd be here. Where she was always was. Peddling donuts and weaving unfruitful day-dreams of Friday at 7:10 a.m.

He didn't even like donuts that much.

Preston Green popped a donut hole into his mouth on his way out of the teachers' lounge, nodding hello at Principal Crowder as he made his way through the throng of jostling students toward his classroom. Something about Lulu's donuts, though… They were special. What had started as a way to get the teachers to like him— the new guy—had easily morphed into a routine he found himself looking forward to every Friday more than he probably should.

"I have good news for you all." Preston raised his voice slightly to be heard above the din of his first-period class settling into their desks. He waited until the scraping of chair legs on linoleum had ceased and they eagerly leaned forward, then he paused for dramatic effect as he set his bag on his chair and unwound his scarf. "It's… Friday."

"Aw, Mr. Green, we already knew that." Claudia Everton, a dark-haired sophomore with a penchant for rock band T-shirts, flopped back in her chair.

"But you didn't know about *these*." He dropped a sack of donut holes on his desk with a flourish. Hopefully Lulu was right, and the gesture would earn him some brownie points. "Courtesy of the town's best donut shop, Oopsy Daisy."

"*Sweet!*" Haylee Richards, a cheerleader with nearly waist-length blond hair, ricocheted off her chair before he could fully get his sentence out. "We love Miss Lulu."

Then a horde of teens flocked his desk, reminding him of seagulls snatching crackers off a beach full of tourists. He fought the urge to cover his head and stayed out of reach as they dispersed back to their desks. The bag was torn down the side and there was nothing but a sprinkling of glaze on his desk to indicate there'd ever been anything there.

Moving on to be a professor next year at a top university in Colorado would be an entirely different experience than teaching at this small-town high school, that was for certain. It wasn't that he hadn't enjoyed working with the kids so far this year—it's just that this job didn't offer the same perks of a higher salary, prestige and respect.

Nor did it allow him a chance to finally catch up to his younger brother Jackson's success.

The only young person who hadn't come forward for grub was Aiden Raines, one of his quieter students who stayed in the back but always made excellent grades. Claudia must have noticed the same, as she twisted in her seat and held up a remaining donut hole. "Yo, Aiden. You want?"

Aiden hesitated, then shook his head. She turned back around with a shrug, stuffing the miniature dessert into her mouth.

Preston leaned against his desk. "Now that I've bribed you all, here's the bad news. We're going to complete our continuing segment on World War II before the holiday break, so expect a test next week."

The class groaned in unison, except for Aiden, who continued staring at his textbook.

"But the auction is next week," Haylee protested, as she leaned forward.

"Yeah, there's a lot to do for the fundraiser." Tori Bryant raised her hand as she spoke, even though no one else ever did. "Remember, it's for a good cause."

"Does that *cause* happen to be getting out of a unit test?" Preston crossed his arms, struggling to keep a straight face while considering their incredibly earnest ones.

"You know the cause is for the school." Tori grinned up at him and he couldn't help but smile back. He loved her story—her friends were all too eager to tell it to anyone new who about how her uncle had adopted her a year ago and saved the animal shelter.

"Remind me about this fundraiser for a cause again?" Preston checked his watch. "Then we really do have to dive into World War II."

"Don't forget, guys, he's new here." Haylee pulled a flyer from her backpack and waved it at him. "This is the annual fundraiser auction. People in the community donate items to be auctioned off and the funds go back into the school for our extracurriculars—like the cheerleading squad."

"And the school band," Claudia added, tapping a rhythm on her desk with a pencil.

"And science club," Tori piped up.

"This year," Haylee, continued, "we're doing something new—we're auctioning off people."

Preston coughed. *"People?"*

A few of the boys in the back row snickered. A football player named Chase smirked. "Are you volunteering, Teach?"

Haylee's eyes widened. "You totally should, Mr. Green! We need eligible bachelors."

"Wait. How do you know he's a bachelor?" Tori frowned.

"Or eligible, for that matter?" Claudia snorted.

He was a bachelor, for certain. Eligible might be debatable—he'd been picked over before. But that wasn't any of their concern. The last thing he needed was someone trying to play matchmaker with their teacher. Besides a smattering of second dates here and there over the years, single was exactly what he'd been ever since his last year of college, when Gabrielle broke up with him for his own brother.

But like World War II, that was ancient history.

Still, he had to know... "What do you mean, auctioning off *people*?"

"Blind dates." Haylee shrugged, as if it were

no big deal. "We think it'll draw a larger crowd. Like one big matchmaking party."

Marketing-wise, it *was* brilliant. Practically, though, it seemed like a recipe for disaster. However, this was Tulip Mound, and as they kept reminding him—he was new here. Maybe things like this worked better in small towns than where he grew up in Wichita.

"So will you?"

He blinked, realizing Haylee, Tori and Claudia were all staring at him with equal intensity. He wasn't even sure which one had spoken. "Will I what?"

"Volunteer," Haylee pressed. "To be auctioned off for a date."

"For a good cause," Tori reminded him. "So… What do you think?"

What did he think? First, he thought that he had officially gotten in over his head with these kids and allowed the conversation to take a wild turn. And second? He thought if his newlywed brother, Jackson, found out that Preston's most recent date had been acquired on an auction block, he'd never live it down.

Oh, and on top of that, he somehow couldn't stop thinking of Lulu and her corny jokes.

"You know what I think?" Preston headed to the dry-erase board mounted on the wall. "I think we should get focused on World War II. Turn your books to page 229…"

He waved off their groans with his marker. One day, they'd understand that sometimes living in the past was more much appealing than considering one's present.

Chapter Two

~

"Hey, Lulu? You really should, like, be on TV or something with these."

She looked up from cleaning fingerprints from the glass display case and squinted at Tori, who perched on a stool at the tasting bar, devouring the last of her Toasted S'more donut. "If I'm ever asked, I'll keep that in mind."

She kept a straight face, but inside, she felt like the Grinch whose heart grew three sizes in one day. The compliments from the students meant more to her than anyone else's—probably because these kids were nothing if not honest.

Claudia, who stood next to Tori at the bar, elbowed the girl in the side. "Trade you a bite for a piece of this eggnog éclair?"

Tori debated a minute, then nodded. "Deal." They swapped treats, while Haylee, sitting delicately on the stool on the other side of Tori,

shook her head at Lulu. "I can't take them anywhere."

"Sure you can. As long as there's food." Claudia grinned, donut crumbs dotting her lips. She
brushed the front of her T-shirt as she looked
over at Lulu. "Do you have any more glazed that
you're going to donate?"

"Your bottomless-pit stomach is not charity,
Claudia." Haylee sniffed. "She has to donate
those to the *real* homeless."

"As it happens, these overcooked a tad and I
was going to throw them away." Lulu set down
her cleaning spray and reached for the discarded
donuts she had yet to toss. "You're welcome to
them."

Claudia's and Tori's eyes gleamed as Haylee
smirked. Then all three reached for one at the
same time.

Strains of a new cover of "Jingle Bell Rock"
drifted through the shop as the daisy clock ticked
away the minutes toward closing time. Lulu always closed at four thirty on weekdays, which
provided the high school kids just enough time
to stop by after school for a snack and demolish
the rest of her stock before she called it a day. In
fact, she enjoyed this hour even more than she
enjoyed 7:10 a.m. on Fridays. Lulu always felt
like she fit in with the kids a little better than she

did fellow adults. Maybe because they matched her natural awkwardness.

The door opened, and Aiden Raines strolled in, a little later than usual, his shoulders hunched inside his navy T-shirt. He didn't come as regularly as the girls did, but usually made it in about once a week.

"Where's your jacket?" Claudia greeted him with a mumble, her mouth full.

Aiden ambled up to the tasting bar. "Don't need it."

"Boys." Haylee sniffed as she smoothed the front of her peacoat. "I'm surprised you're not wearing shorts, too."

"Guys have higher resting metabolic rates. That's why they're not as cold as we are." Tori twisted to face them, her expression serious. "Look it up. It's science."

"Don't worry, Aiden, I won't let them experiment on you." Lulu offered the teen boy a smile as the playlist switched songs to "Last Christmas." "What'll it be today?"

"I'm good." He leaned against the empty stool on the end of the row and fiddled with the fake poinsettia.

Did his stomach just growl? Lulu frowned. He probably didn't have any spending money today and didn't want to embarrass himself in front of the girls. She casually motioned toward the donut tray in front of Claudia. "That's too bad. I was really hoping to get rid of these glazed, here. They overcooked and are useless to me."

His eyes lit up, but his lips pressed together as if attempting to hide his eagerness. He shook back his dark hair from his forehead. "I guess I could help."

"I'd be super grateful if you did." Lulu slid a napkin toward him, watching from the corner of her eye as he eagerly scooped up two. Then he went for a third before he finished chewing the first.

"Boys," Haylee said again, shaking her head as she wiped the counter in front of her with an antibacterial wipe. "I've been trying to ask you a question, Lulu, but this crew makes it hard."

"They're all chewing now. I think it's safe." Lulu crossed her arms and leaned over the counter in front of the teen.

"So." Haylee clasped her hands in front of her, all business. "You'd do anything for us, right?"

"Hmm. I get the feeling you're talking about more than free donuts."

"Yeah, well…" Haylee smiled her brightest cheerleader smile. "The squad is responsible for finding people willing to be auctioned off at the fundraiser next week on blind dates. And I thought you could do it."

"Me?" Lulu's voice came out in a squeak, and

she cleared her throat. "I'm happy to donate donuts, but I don't know—"

"It's just one date." Haylee's voice turned pleading. "We really need some volunteers. It's for a good cause." She paused, then sat up even straighter. "Oh! I almost forgot. You get to choose a charity of your choice to receive half the funds that you raise. Say someone wins a date with you for twenty dollars, then ten would go to the Haven Project or whatever cause you wanted."

Twenty dollars—was that all she'd go for? What if no one even bid *that*? Talk about the opportunity for pure humiliation. She opened her mouth to protest, then swallowed back her immediate dismissal. This was important to Haylee—and it would be nice to raise money for the Haven Project. Even if she didn't earn very much, her participating could at least raise awareness for the organization in general.

But then she'd have to actually go on a *date*.

She gnawed on her lower lip, debating what to do. She hated to tell these kids no. Plus, it wasn't like Tulip Mound was crawling with a lot of singles. They probably needed anyone who was available. Practically everyone on staff at Tulip Mound High was married.

She briefly wondered if Preston would be auctioned off. He didn't wear a ring—she'd noticed that key fact the first day he'd come in—but a lot of men these days didn't. She hesitated, running her hands down the front of her apron as a new thought dawned. What if he *wasn't* single? Horror flamed in her cheeks.

"Are you okay?" Haylee arched thin eyebrows at her. "Maybe you should sit down."

"No, I'm fine." Lulu fanned herself with a paper menu. He *had* to be unattached. He wouldn't have flirted—well, maybe he hadn't. She had, though. Or rather, tried. An image of herself clicking the tongs and rattling off ridiculous jokes flooded her mind, bringing a fresh wave of heat surging into her neck.

"Seriously, if the thought of volunteering for the auction is going to send you to the hospital, I withdraw my offer." Haylee frowned.

Some of the tension crowding Lulu's shoulders eased. It was sweet of the younger girl to be so concerned—

"I mean, we need healthy people on that stage, you know? No fainting under the lights or anything. That would be bad for business." The teen crossed her arms over her chest, looking something like a stern schoolteacher herself.

"Okay." The word fumbled from her lips before Lulu could rescind it. That's what she did, right? She helped people. And in this case, she would be helping Haylee meet her volunteer quota *and* aiding the Haven Project. Not to mention the school. She could get through one date for the sake of a good cause. "I'll do it."

"You *will*?" Haylee's expression suddenly rivaled the glow of the twinkle lights draped across the outside awning. "And you'll bring donuts, too, right?"

Maybe that would help increase her bids. She nodded. "Of course."

Haylee squealed and reached over the bar to hug Lulu. "Thank you! I bet you'll bring in the big bucks." She pulled back slightly, examining Lulu's face at close range. "And don't worry. I have a pink lip gloss you can borrow."

Spin class was looking better and better.

Saturday mornings in Tulip Mound looked like something out of a snow globe.

Preston tugged the ends of his winter scarf down as he strolled down Peach Street, the effect of the brisk wind streaming between the buildings dulled by the warm afternoon sun. Wreaths decorated with crimson bows adorned each streetlamp he passed, and the store windows boasted a variety of red and green holiday cheer. Santa waved from the lawn of the community college's coffee shop, and Preston waved back as an elf in striped leggings ushered the next kid in line forward to present his holiday wish.

The small-town charm was nice, compared with where he grew up farther west in Wichita. No exhaust, no overt traffic noises, no need for multiple locks on the doors. But Tulip Mound didn't offer what he needed. As soon as he finished his year of high school experience, he could reapply for the professor's gig in Denver, Colorado, and move up the ladder. Apparently, he'd tried to start one rung too soon. But the board who interviewed him earlier last spring assured him that his chances at securing the position he wanted would triple if he had this year behind him...

Preston's phone buzzed, and he glanced down at the lit screen in his hand. A text from his mom.

CALL ME.

After his father's prior run with cancer, his heart still jump-started a little at his mother's careless way of wording her texts. But that was all over with—his dad had been in remission three years now. Preston called her back, continuing his walk as it rang twice before she answered.

"Good morning."

He kicked lightly at the curb as he paused his stroll. "Hey, Mom."

Water ran in the background. She was probably at the sink, doing breakfast dishes. Mom still got up and made a big breakfast for his dad every Saturday,

"You know I'm not one to guilt-trip, right?"

"Right." Not intentionally, anyway. His mother just liked everything neat and tidy, tucked into carefully formed boxes. Unfortunately, Preston's dating life had never found its way into one of them. Hopefully this wasn't another one of her not-so-subtle attempts to set him up with a friend's daughter. Ever since Jackson married Gabrielle this past summer, she'd upped her efforts.

She continued. "I was talking with your father, and we just wanted to know… Are you *sure* you can't come home for more than just Christmas weekend? Aren't you off work the entire week?"

Almost three weeks, really, because of New Year's and the school's generous holiday calendar, but he hated to remind her of that part. "I'll be there for Christmas, Mom. Don't worry. You know I'm still trying to get settled in here."

"Of course." His mother's voice brightened. "That's exactly what I thought. So I have a better idea."

He checked the street for cars, then crossed to

the other side, frowning. This couldn't be headed in a good direction...

"We're coming to you!"

There it was. His heart stammered, and he spoke fast. "What do you mean, Mom? I'm perfectly capable of driving back home to see you for the holidays. Just like we planned." *Stick to the plan...stick to the plan...*

Dishes clanked, then the water shut off. "It'll be better this way. We'll come to you and stay a few days. Have a nice Christmas meal in your new house and see your town. It looks downright charming on social media."

Since when did his mom have social media? He furrowed his brow. "Mom, I don't—"

"We'll get a hotel, so don't worry about putting us up." Cabinet doors squeaked open. "And, of course, we'll have to do it before Christmas, because of your brother's work schedule."

Wait. His stomach clenched. "What does you and Dad visiting me for Christmas have to do with Jackson's work?" Somehow his superhero of a brother managed to run a successful construction company that had expanded into three additional cities, and he still wasn't even a workaholic. Meanwhile, Preston would be up until close to midnight grading papers.

"Well, they're coming, too, of course."

Of course. Preston's shoulders dropped an

inch at the sudden load. *They.* He wasn't used to hearing Jackson referred to in multiples. But now he had a wife. As the Bible stated, two had become one, and now Jackson was part of a team.

The question remained, why did it have to be *that* one? It wasn't that Preston missed Gabrielle, specifically. Hindsight had easily proved they wouldn't have been a good long-term match. It was more that Jackson beat him at something else. His little brother, permanently showing him up. Professionally, romantically… It never ended. Part of why Preston had moved to Tulip Mound in the first place was to have some space from his brother's success constantly flaunted in his face, while everyone in the family threw pity dates Preston's way.

It'd be a lot easier to be single right now if his career was further along. He just needed one year…

His mother cleared her throat, obviously trying to fill the strained silence. "Have you talked to your brother lately?"

"Not really." More like not at all since the wedding, but that was a detail she didn't need. His mom tended to be overprotective and controlling, and she didn't need any more ammo in that department.

His mom sighed. "Well, in that case, Christmas

dinner will be good for all of us." She used her *don't argue with me* voice, and Preston didn't dare.

Preston clenched his jaw. Apparently, this was inevitable. "Okay, Mom. I'll see you guys soon." He hung up after they said their goodbyes.

Showing his parents around Tulip Mound wasn't the problem—though a big family visit to see his new home seemed fruitless as he planned to leave in less than a year. He'd only rented the split-level cottage he'd found, which had come partially furnished, and still had a few boxes in the under-the-stairs closet he hadn't bothered unpacking because hopefully he'd have to just do it again next summer.

In the grand scheme of things, it was the dinner with Jackson that weighed on him the most. The table set for five, instead of six. The pointed remarks of how Mom ran into so-and-so the other day, and her daughter was recently divorced, and didn't Preston remember how pretty she was?

The door of the general store on Peach Street suddenly swung wide, narrowly missing him as he paused under the awning. A woman barreled out, juggling an armful of bags and a sturdy box, and stepped directly on his loafer. "I'm so sorry!"

He caught her elbow, steadying them both, and realized it was Lulu. "Don't be. It's a welcome distraction." He stepped back, and his mood instantly brightened as he took in her chaotic presence. Her hair, mussed under a bright crochet beanie, stuck out at several angles, and her jacket slipped off one shoulder as she struggled beneath the weight of her load. "Here, let me help you."

He easily hoisted the box out of her arms, and she thanked him as she adjusted first her hat and then the bags hanging over her elbows. "I really didn't think this through when I volunteered to pick up the order. I should have brought a wagon."

"Indeed. Or a mule." He smiled. "Where am I taking this?"

"Fern Avenue, if you don't mind. It's two blocks south." She gestured down the street. "Are you sure you're not busy?"

"I was heading for coffee, but I can detour first." He shrugged as he adjusted his grip. "What is all this, anyway?"

She brushed at hair still lingering in her face. "It's for the Haven Project. We're working on the Home for the Holidays build and ran out of some basics."

"I wondered if this was actually a load of bricks," he joked as he fell into step beside her. "I'm surprised you're not working today. I would think Saturdays would be a busy time in the donut industry."

"Oh, it is. I have a college student who helps me out. She usually does the Saturday morning shift so I can work with the Haven Project." Lulu waved to Santa as they passed back by. "That's Clyde, by the way. I hope that doesn't ruin the holiday magic for you."

Preston chuckled as another layer of stress from his mother's news rolled off his back. "Not at all."

Lulu glanced up at him, her eyes wide beneath her hat. "So what did you mean by a welcome distraction?"

He hadn't meant to say that part out loud. He hesitated. "Let's just say I had spiraled into some worry that isn't fitting for such a beautiful Saturday morning."

"Fair enough." She didn't push, which impressed him. The few women he'd attempted to date since college had apparently never heard the expression "curiosity killed the cat" and had no qualms about quizzing him on all his innermost thoughts. It was part of what turned him off to the idea of a blind date with someone now—he didn't want to confide in a stranger. Didn't want to start the whole exhausting process of getting to know someone new. Especially not until he got his *real* career moving.

They rounded the corner of Peach onto Main Street, and already, the sounds of hammering and electric drills met his ears. "Tell me more about this Home for the Holidays project you mentioned."

One of the bags hanging on Lulu's arm swung hard into his hip, but she either pretended not to notice or didn't. He hid his smile as she answered.

"It's my favorite nonprofit. The Haven Project helps build or restore low-income housing, and once a year, they construct a brand-new house and do a lottery drawing for everyone in a sixty-mile radius who enters and qualifies in the lower-income bracket."

"So you're saying someone will win a house this Christmas?"

"A home for the holidays." Lulu nodded with pride.

"Wow." Preston followed her lead onto Fern Avenue as the construction sounds grew louder. "And you help...build the house?" He would have never pictured his favorite donut peddler swinging a hammer, but now, walking briskly beside her as she carried an armful of bags to a jobsite, well, maybe he could. The fact that she lit up like a Christmas tree just mentioning the project also spoke volumes.

"Sometimes it's more like passing out donuts and Band-Aids, but I usually find something to contribute." Lulu stopped in front of the construction site, where the framing was in progress. "I like to give back to good causes... So does my mom. She's actually away this entire year, working for the Haven Project International. They're building houses in Bolivia, Ecuador, Colombia... I forget where else."

"So it's a family affair."

"She inspires me." Lulu smiled. "Plus, I think of it sort of like my mission field. My church gave up trying to get me to teach Sunday school or volunteer in the nursery years ago." She let out a little snort, as if remembering some calamity she didn't feel inclined to share.

Preston grinned. Knowing Lulu the little he did already, he could only imagine. "What church do you go to?"

"Grace Community, back on the corner." She swung one arm to point behind them, and the same bag slammed into his hip again. This time her eyes widened, but she didn't acknowledge it. "What about you?"

"I've only visited there once since I moved here. I tried the church on Main Street a few weeks ago, but it wasn't a good fit." He hadn't seen Lulu at Grace that one Sunday he'd attended, but then again, he hadn't known to look for her. "I might try your service again tomorrow."

Maybe. Somehow, the thought of Lulu being

there made it seem more palatable. Sort of less likely for God to notice him and therefore realize how much he'd been *out* of church the past few years.

"Some of your students go there, too. I've been trying to get them to volunteer with me at the Haven Project." She shrugged. "I'm successful about half the time."

He let out a chuckle. "Hey, from what I've seen so far as an educator, fifty percent is still pretty successful when it comes to teens and commitment. Good for you for staying on them."

"I think it's beneficial for everyone to volunteer for programs like this occasionally. People need to realize how other people live, you know?" Lulu met his gaze, then quickly looked away, as if she'd startled herself. "Thanks for the help."

"Anytime." He transferred the box back into her arms.

"Okay." She glanced back at him, a mixture of awkward and sheepish, then started to wave before apparently remembering she couldn't spare a hand from the box. It tipped dangerously to the left. He reached to steady it, but she'd already caught it. "Bye, then."

Preston couldn't help but watch her beeline toward the site with her load, her short dark hair sticking out from all sides of her beanie, and tried and failed to suppress a smile. He liked Lulu's sense of humor. Being around her was easy. And she seemed comfortable with him, too—until she suddenly wasn't. He shook his head, having no idea what that was about. Hopefully it wasn't anything he did or said that made her uncomfortable. He'd much rather make her laugh.

He hesitated, then called after her. "Hey, Lulu!"

Turning around, she lifted her chin in silent acknowledgment.

He pointed toward the jobsite. "What did the contractor do when I told him I didn't want carpeted steps?"

Lulu tilted her head. "What?"

"He gave me a blank *stair*."

Her responding snort and eye roll made him grin the whole way to the coffee shop.

Chapter Three

"Don't worry." Haylee reached over and adjusted a lock of hair draped across Lulu's forehead. "My lip gloss looks great on you."

"That's not the part I'm worried about." Lulu glanced around the hectic backstage area of the Tulip Mound High auditorium. Cheerleaders clad in their red-and-white uniforms scurried around a handful of teachers reading over scripts and fixing the microphones clipped onto their shirt collars. Preston, thankfully, was not one of them. The whole evening was turning out to be a much bigger event than Lulu had anticipated when she'd first agreed to be auctioned off for a good cause.

And thinking of her chosen charity, the Haven Project, only made her remember Preston walking her to the jobsite last weekend. She'd only seen him one time since, as she never found him at church last Sunday. He'd come in Oopsy Daisy for his typical Friday order that morning, but they didn't get to talk because of an unexpected rush of customers. She'd simply boxed up his usual, handed him his receipt, then said "you, too" as he told her thanks.

"Well, my lip gloss is perfect, but you might have overdone the blush." Haylee frowned, swiping at Lulu's flushed cheeks.

She swatted her away.

"Anyway, I doubt you'll trip, if that's what you're concerned about." Haylee's eyes grew serious as she brushed a piece of lint off Lulu's shoulder. "But if you do, remember to cradle the donut box."

Lulu briefly closed her eyes, her fingers tightening around her carefully crafted box of holiday-themed treats. How had tripping not occurred to her? "Okay, *now* I'm worried."

"You'll do great!" Tori bounded up to them, her ponytail swinging across the back of her puffy jacket. "I wish I could be auctioned for a date! Sounds like fun."

"It's only fun if someone bids." Claudia joined them with a knowing grin. Her long-sleeve trademark T-shirt featured the Beatles tonight. "Also, this whole concept is kind of old-fashioned, isn't it? Bidding on women for a date?" She scrunched up her nose, which Lulu noticed for the first time had a tiny silver stud piercing.

"Old-fashioned is quaint. Besides, it's not just women. Men are being auctioned, too. We just couldn't find as many of them willing to do it." Haylee gripped Lulu's shoulders and turned her around, toward stage left. "Get ready. It's almost your turn."

Lulu swallowed hard. This was it. She waited for her cue, palms growing slick on the daisy-themed donut box as she suddenly doubted her outfit. Maybe she should have worn jeans or something simple, not her favorite bohemian-style maxi dress. What if she was too off-putting? Didn't men prefer understated? Neal always had.

Not that she knew much about fashion, anyway. If she thought about it too long, she'd remember all those childhood days of her pants being a little too short, of her sleeves exposing her wrists, of her classmate's smirks...but no, this wasn't the time to stumble down Memory Lane.

Tori appeared at her side with a beaming smile. "If you get nervous, just keep holding up those donuts. No one will be able to resist you."

At this point, Lulu wasn't sure if she was more afraid of someone bidding or *not* bidding. Both outcomes seemed problematic. But if they did, it was just one date, right?

Still, the snide barbs from Neal's parents pelted her thoughts. Ironic, how his parents rejected her essentially because of her donuts, but right now, that's all the teens seemed confident Lulu had to work with.

How could she be too much and not enough, all at once?

Her stomach pinched as an image of Preston filled her mind, his teasing grin as he bantered with a joke of his own, the way he'd easily carried her heavy load for her to the jobsite, the manner in which he'd spoken of the teens in his class. She felt different around Preston, more comfortable…though she still embarrassed herself plenty. Maybe he was different from Neal, but it didn't matter. It wasn't like Preston had shown any interest in her, other than being friendly and chivalrous.

All she knew for sure was that men were too risky. Too inconsistent. Maybe not all of them, of course—she hated stereotypes and labeling—but apparently, she wasn't very good at identifying the good ones.

And her heart just couldn't take any more cracks.

"…which brings this young lady's total to seventy-five dollars!" Principal Crowder's voice grew loud from the other side of the curtain, where she played emcee for the evening. The crowd in the auditorium burst into applause. "That's our highest bid so far!"

Lulu's heart plummeted. "Seventy-five dollars?" She'd been hoping to land fifty, at best.

"Yikes. It'll be hard to follow that." Claudia crossed her arms and *tsked* her sympathy.

"Don't listen to her." Tori gave Lulu a comforting side hug. "It's not a competition."

"Actually, it kind of is," Haylee corrected as she gave Lulu's hair one last fluff. "But all for a good cause! You got this."

She didn't, but Lulu headed toward the stage anyway as one of the backstage hands pulled the curtain aside for her. The bright spotlights swallowed her up, and she squared her shoulders as she reminded herself that her worth was not determined by one auction. She was doing this for the kids. For the Haven Project.

And maybe a teeny bit for herself.

Preston sat in the school's auditorium, shifting his weight on the uncomfortable wooden seat as Christmas music blared through the staticky speakers overhead. He'd come to the fundraiser tonight to support the school, despite the stack of papers waiting to be graded back at his cottage. Since he refused to be auctioned off himself, he felt attending was the least he could do.

Then he'd had an idea on the way here, and

while it was completely ridiculous, he couldn't quite brush it off.

What if he placed a bid on a date for Christmas dinner?

He hooked one ankle over the other in the cramped aisle before him, mulling the idea around as he alternated between rejecting it and embracing it. The thought had its perks. Bringing someone to Christmas dinner would not only help him save face in front of his newly-wed brother, it would also eliminate any potential matchmaking efforts from his mom. If his family believed he was already seeing someone, they'd back off and maybe they could enjoy their meal.

It was tempting.

But the downside was that he didn't want to bring a stranger, either. That would involve a whole host of uncomfortable moments, especially if it was someone he worked with at the school.

It seemed risky. But it also might be his only option.

Having come no further to deciding, Preston watched as the next volunteer strode onto the stage to join Principal Crowder in the spotlight. Then the woman proceeded to trip, and the entire room gasped as she rightened herself and successfully held up a box of—donuts?

Lulu.

His eyes widened. *Lulu* was being auctioned? On second thought, he should have expected the kids to hit her up to volunteer...and he should have known she'd never resist them.

He smiled, feeling oddly proud of her as she played off her misstep with a little curtsy. The crowd applauded, and he joined in. She looked different tonight, having styled her hair and traded her apron for a flowing dress that complimented her slender frame.

Scott Mitchell, the ninth-grade science teacher whose classroom was just down the wing from his own, leaned over from the chair next to Preston. "Hey, that's the lady who makes those donuts you're always bringing in on Fridays, isn't it?"

Preston nodded. "Are you going to bid?" A flare lit his chest at the thought, and he frowned. That was weird.

"Not sure my wife would go for that." Scott laughed as he held up his left hand, indicating the thick silver band.

Right. Not much of the faculty was single, and several of the teachers had already bid.

"I'd bid just for the donuts, though. They're amazing," Scott added before settling back in his seat.

Wait a minute.

He could bid on Lulu.

"We'll start the bidding at fifteen dollars," Principal Crowder prompted, the older woman's smile growing wide. "Trust me, gentlemen, you don't want to miss a treat from Oopsy Daisy. You're getting good food *and* good company with this opportunity."

"I'll bid fifteen!" An anonymous arm, clad in a black sleeve, rose from the front of the room.

Relief practically poured off Lulu's expression. She dipped her head in acknowledgment, even as she visibly blew out her breath.

Principal Crowder glanced from left to right across the room. "Fifteen dollars! Do we have twenty?"

This was his chance. Heart pounding, Preston started to raise his arm, but his seat neighbor beat him to it.

"Twenty dollars!" Scott volunteered. Then he shot Preston a sheepish look. "I'll bring my wife, don't worry. She loves those donuts."

Preston's phone buzzed with an incoming call, and the distraction cost him another round of bidding between Scott and the black-sleeved bidder in the front row. He craned his head to see who the man was, that weird flare rising in his chest again.

"We have fifty! What about sixty?" Principal Crowder asked as the crowd hummed in surprise.

Lulu gripped her donut box, her feeble smile looking like she was torn between celebrating the escalating bids and being sick. Preston hesitated. Would she misunderstand his intentions if he bid on her? He didn't want to lead her on. Their casual friendship was a blessing, and he'd hate to complicate it.

But if he was going to bring a date, it'd be nice to have someone he was already familiar with by his side.

Then the man in the front row raised his bid to one hundred dollars.

"One hundred dollars! A record for the night!" Principal Crowder grew giddy as she gestured wildly toward Lulu, who still clutched her donut box as her face blanched as white as the daisy on the package. "Do we have one hundred and fifteen?"

Preston started to raise his hand, then lowered it. That was a lot of money to save face at a family dinner. Then he imagined Jackson's smirk across the table at the empty chair beside him. Envisioned Gabrielle's awkward smile and his father's disappointed shoulder clap. Imagined his mother's endless list of potential setups.

Decision made. He shot his hand up high.

"Two hundred dollars."

The crowd stilled, and Principal Crowder's mouth dropped open. Preston glanced between her and Lulu, not sure which of them looked the most shocked, and drew in a deep breath as Lulu's gaze locked onto his.

So much for no complications.

Lulu searched the thickening crowd backstage for Preston, clutching her box of donuts so tightly the corners of the white cardboard were starting to fold. Two hundred dollars.

Two. Hundred. Dollars.

She wasn't sure what to think about that and didn't know what to do with the thoughts if they ever came, so she gladly stayed numb, holding on to her donuts for dear life. She scanned the laughing, mingling group of adults and teenagers around her behind the stage curtains, heart clamoring into her throat as she waited for Preston to come claim his prize.

Her.

Principal Crowder's laugh rose over the rest of the din, jolting Lulu's shot nerves. Where was Preston? What if he didn't show? She swallowed hard. In her experience, men were wishy-washy. He'd probably recognized his error, maybe had gotten carried away with the competition, and was trying to claim an audience with Principal Crowder right now to undo his mistake. No one in their right mind would pay that much for an evening with her.

She tried to prepare her heart for the rejection in advance. It's not that she wanted the date, anyway.

Then a man in a dark jacket stepped out of the way of the stage, and Preston filled the space behind him. Lulu rolled in her bottom lip. He was here. Purposefully walking toward her.

He hadn't changed his mind.

Her stomach flipped, and she wasn't sure if it was from pure joy or true dread. She didn't date. What was she doing? Of all the things for those kids to talk her into…

Then Preston's gaze found hers and locked in, and his eyes crinkled slightly at the sides. He lifted one shoulder in a sheepish shrug, and the tight knot in Lulu's stomach unwound a few inches.

She started to raise one shaky palm in a wave, when Claudia appeared directly in front of her and slapped Lulu's raised hand in a high five. "Right on!"

Before Lulu could recover, Haylee's wide-eyed expression filled her peripheral. "Well. That was a record." The younger girl shook her head, seemingly as equally stunned as Lulu over the course of the night's events. "I have to admit, I really didn't expect that."

"Why not? We know Lulu is awesome." Claudia slung one arm around Lulu's shoulders. "Plus she comes with a bonus." She tapped the donut box with her other hand. "Who could resist these?"

"Maybe it was the lip gloss…" Haylee's voice trailed off as she tilted her head and studied Lulu. She nodded briskly, as if deciding the logic proved true. "It's called Peachy Keen. I'll send you the link."

Lulu opened her mouth to protest, knowing she'd never wear it again, but was interrupted as Tori sidled up to them.

"I knew you could do it." The younger girl smiled sweetly.

Finally, a genuine cheerleader. Lulu's shoulders relaxed. "Thank you—"

"I also told Uncle Blake to be ready to bid on you just in case no one else did."

Preston must have heard her as he drew nearer, because he clearly tried and failed to suppress the grin spreading across his face. Lulu stifled a groan. This might be worse than tripping on stage.

He cleared his throat. "I'm glad for your uncle's sake that wasn't necessary, Tori."

The girls turned to face him, their expressions sheepish. "Hi, Mr. Green."

He smiled. "Ladies? If I may have a moment?"

"Sure." Tori frowned. "Wait… With us? Or her?" She pointed at Lulu.

' "He means *her*, of course." Haylee rolled her eyes. "Come on."

"Donuts wait for no man." Claudia patted Preston on the shoulder as she scooted out of the way. "All yours, Teach."

Haylee followed, plucking Tori's sleeve to pull her with them, leaving Preston and Lulu standing semi-alone as the crowd began to pour down the short stairs and away from backstage.

"You came." Lulu hadn't meant to say that out loud, but that was the story of her life, wasn't it? She handed over the box, glad her hands had finally stopped shaking. "I mean, here you go. Your winnings."

"This is definitely the most expensive dessert I ever bought." He smiled, his gaze gentle as it rested directly on her. "But all for a good cause, right?"

Lulu nodded. "Right." Because that's why he had bid on her. For the cause. And maybe because of his sweet tooth.

"You did great up there."

"I tripped."

"I saw. But you played it off well." That little quirky, half smile of his was back, and it shot the same jolt of awareness through Lulu that she got every time he came into Oopsy Daisy.

Was he attracted to her, or was this just a staff thing…his doing his part for the school and the kids he taught? She wasn't sure which option brought the most anxiety, and she desperately wished she had the donut box to clutch again.

Preston looked around, his expression shifting slightly. "Listen, we should go talk. Do you have a minute?"

"Of course." She drew a tight breath. Here it came. The clarification of what he was after. A true date with her...or an expensive snack for a good cause?

"Don't worry, I plan to share." He held up the box and quirked an eyebrow. "Unless you're sick of these already?"

She quickly shook her head, then studied his broad, jacket-clad back as he turned to lead the way out of the auditorium. She wasn't sick of them.

But oh, she wished she was.

Chapter Four

The park bench outside in the school courtyard pressed cold through the thin fabric of Lulu's dress as she took a seat at Preston's insistence. She'd left her jacket in the car because when she'd pulled up at Tulip Mound High earlier in the evening, she'd been such a sweaty mess she didn't want to consider wearing another layer. Now, though…

But she didn't even have time to shiver before he draped his coat over her shoulders. "Thank you." She adjusted the collar around her neck. He was always the gentleman. But hadn't Neal been, too?

It was silly to compare them. Why did she keep doing that?

The glow from the courtyard lamps glinted off Preston's watch as he reached up and ran a hand through his dark hair. "Sorry about this. I didn't think it all the way through."

"Which part? The cold, or spending that much money on me?" She snorted before catching herself, then stifled a groan. Way to make him regret his investment. She snuggled into the coat a little farther, hiding.

But Preston's eyes held zero judgment and a lot of amusement as he leaned back on the bench, shifting slightly to face her. "Both, honestly."

"That *was* a lot of money." Oy. She still couldn't quite seem to say the right thing, so she opened the box of doughnuts and extended her offering to distract him. "Here. You pick first. I have to warn you, though, there's no basic chocolate or glazed. I went for my gourmet recipes."

He leaned forward, squinting at the box of goodies drenched partly in shadow. "Is that one caramel?" He pointed.

She nodded. "With apple filling."

"Sold." He scooped the dessert up with two fingers.

"It's better hot—tastes just like a pie then." She took a white chocolate peppermint donut for herself, then tucked the flaps back into the box. "But it'll do."

"It's perfect, trust me."

The deep timbre of his voice seeped through the cold and warmed her all the way through. And yet… She had to know. "Can I ask you a question?"

The slamming of car doors sounded across the still courtyard, echoing from the parking lot around the corner of the school's main hall. The crowd was beginning to disperse, which suddenly felt like a ticking bomb on their conversation. She fidgeted on the bench. "So why didn't you participate?"

His gaze met hers, that trademark easygoing spark never leaving his eyes. "Is that the question you wanted to ask?"

Just looking at him made her want to smile back. He was so easy to talk to. All of this should have been much more awkward than it was, though she was certainly doing her part to make it so.

Lulu shook her head. "No, that wasn't my original question. Do I have to pick just one?"

"Seems only fair if you did…since I'm the one who *technically* brought you here to ask *you* a question."

Her heart hammered. Right. The date discussion. Was he wanting one? Maybe this counted, instead. Lulu's eyes widened. Was she on a date right now and didn't even know it? That seemed like something that would happen to her.

She swallowed hard.

"So, ladies first. What's your looming question?" Preston's blue eyes, unblinking, held her gaze steady and managed to still her internal gymnastics. Each time he talked to her it was as if he had all the time in the world. This was definitely a man she could be friends with.

Just friends, of course.

She probably shouldn't even ask her question. The conversation was going well, and there was no telling how she might mess it up from here if she followed her instincts. And yet it sat there on her lips, begging to be asked.

She took a deep breath before she chickened out. "Why didn't you just bid one hundred and fifteen dollars?"

Preston coughed, hard, as if the donut had personally attacked him. He pounded his chest with his fist, then croaked a response. "What do you mean?"

"I think you're supposed to raise your arm over your head if you're choking."

He sputtered. "That's an old wives' tale."

Lulu shrugged. "Better safe than sorry." Maybe this was a sign she shouldn't explain herself. She rolled in her bottom lip, not wanting him to keep choking, of course, but thinking how much easier the rest of the conversation would be if he did.

"I'm fine." He coughed again, his eyes watering. "Wrong pipe. Go ahead."

Apparently, she was too far in now to back out. She met his eyes, still slightly glassy from his coughing fit. "You bid two hundred dollars. But the next natural bid was a lot lower than that."

"I had competition."

"Ah." She narrowed her eyes. "So you're competitive?" Also like Neal.

Oops.

He shrugged. "No more than the next guy."

So maybe not like Neal. "But you wanted to win badly enough to—"

He tugged the donut box back from her lap. "I had my reasons."

Ah. Of course—the donuts. That made more sense. Lulu was a good cook. She knew her donuts were legendary around town. So why did the constant validation of that fact feel more discouraging than complimentary?

They needed to get this discussion over with. It was too cold to go that deep into personal speculation. She pulled the jacket tighter around her shoulders, refusing to breathe in the scent of his masculine cologne. "Okay, your turn. You said you came to ask me something."

"I did." His gaze grew serious as it lingered back on hers. "It's a little wacky. I guess that's why I've been stalling."

Oh, no. He *was* going to ask her out. Her heart pounded hard beneath the flimsy fabric of her dress. What else could it be? Why else would he have sat here this long with her? All the signs clearly pointed to him wanting to take her on a *real*—

"I need you to pretend to be my girlfriend for Christmas dinner."

Her shoulders stiffened. Make that a *fake*... date.

He probably should have eased her into it.

Lulu's face paled, though maybe it was just the impression from the lamplight above them. Or from the chilly night. He gently touched her jacket-clad arm. "Did you hear me?"

He was an idiot. He should turn back. But he was two hundred dollars poorer, and his family *was* still coming, so he didn't exactly have a choice here.

"I heard." She dipped her head in acknowledgment. "I'm just trying to understand."

He didn't blame her. "Look, I know it's odd, but if you could just hear me out…"

"I'm listening."

She was cold. Her nose was turning red.

"Let's walk while we talk." He stood, tugging gently at her elbow, then waited while she wrapped herself more fully inside his jacket. That dress was pretty, but she had to be freezing. "We can head to the parking lot by cutting through the school, and that will let you warm up for a minute inside."

They began the trek back across the lawn to the auditorium, leaves crunching under their shoes. How to begin? He took a breath. "I have a younger brother."

She clutched his coat with both hands. "That must be nice. I'm an only child."

He hesitated, not wanting to dump his entire family history on her during one brief walk. "Let's just say it has its pros and cons." To put it mildly. "Right now there's a big con I'm dealing with."

"Oh?"

"My family—my parents and my brother and his new wife—are coming for an early Christmas dinner that I'm apparently hosting here in my new, *downright charming town.*" He emphasized his mother's words.

"We are that." Lulu grinned up at him, and his confidence surged. Maybe she'd go for this plan after all.

"I don't know your relationship with your parents, but—" did her face just darken, or was that a passing shadow "—mine can be interesting."

Her expression settled into something neutral he couldn't quite read. "I'm pretty close with my mom. We just don't get to talk much right now with her traveling abroad."

Right. He waited, but she didn't offer any information on her father. And the wall he felt going up between them didn't invite questioning.

"Go on," she prompted. "We're not here to talk about me."

"I'd like to, sometime."

She shot him a glance, also unreadable, and he felt the urge to get to the point.

"As I was saying, I know my mother means well, but she's eternally trying to set me up with her friends' daughters, and..." His voice trailed off.

Lulu watched the ground as they closed the distance to the auditorium back entrance, giving him no further insight into her processing. "And?"

He opened the heavy door and ushered her inside the heated space. "It's extra awkward now that my baby brother is married."

Understanding filled her eyes as she finally turned to him. "I see."

"Do you?" He dared to hope.

"You want a break from the pressure."

Relief surged through him as they continued walking through the school. "Yes! If you and I could just act like we're dating for this one dinner, it would make my parents happy, give me that break and..."

"And let you save face in front of your brother."

She nodded, turning toward him under the fluorescent-lit hallway. "I don't have a sibling, like I said. But I get it."

"So you'll do it?" He had to know for sure.

"I do owe you a date." She motioned toward the donut box in his hands, then shrugged. She didn't look completely thrilled with the idea, but she wasn't protesting, either.

For a moment, he wondered if she'd have ever agreed to go on a real date instead a fake one—bid or no bid. Her statement sounded riddled with obligation. Maybe she wasn't interested in spending any extra time with him and was disappointed that he'd bid on her. That would make sense, considering the questions she'd asked.

A tinge of disappointment swept through him, but he shook it aside. Whether she was open to real dating or not was a moot point. He wasn't staying in town longer than this school year, and besides, they barely knew each other outside of their weekly interactions in her shop.

And just because she looked cute tucked into his oversize jacket didn't mean he was attracted to her. He'd let his mom and her matchmaking get in his head, that was all.

Preston cleared his throat. "Are you sure? I don't want you to do anything you're not comfortable with."

Her somewhat guarded expression melted

slightly. "I'm sure. I know what it's like to be considered something you're not and want to prove that to the other person. So I'll help."

"I really appreciate it."

Lulu lifted her chin. "There's one condition."

He should have known that'd been too easy. "Fair enough."

That passion that had lit her eyes the other day immediately filled her expression once more. "In exchange, you volunteer with me at the Haven Project."

The building project for low-income families? He'd never done anything like that before.

As if sensing his hesitation, she barreled on. "They're really behind on the deadline right now, so we need all the elbow grease we can get to be ready for Christmas Eve."

He shifted his weight from one leg to the other, a dozen thoughts rolling through his head. "I'm not very handy with tools." What little he did know came from YouTube videos, and his results with attempting house repairs over the years had ended with a 50 percent success rate. Apparently, Jackson had scooped up all those genes, too, and turned them into a construction empire.

"You don't have to be. The crew can teach you, and there's plenty to do that isn't dangerous and is still a big help."

He wasn't afraid of hard work. But he had planned to spend a portion of his break taking an online course that would help his credentials when he applied for the professor position. With all the midterm grading he also needed to do during his holiday time off, he wasn't sure how he'd manage all of it.

Lulu tapped his arm. "Plus, several of your students volunteer. It'd be good for them to see you interacting with the community this way. Earn you some of those teacher brownie points you were wanting."

The fact that she even remembered he'd said that impressed him. She was a good listener *and* retained things about other people. And she was right. That would be good for them to see, and he was selfish if he did anything differently. He could squeeze in the online course in January or February, instead.

His mom was really going to like Lulu.

"If that's your condition, I'm in." Besides, he really needed this dinner. "One fake Christmas date in exchange for…how many volunteer hours?"

She scrunched her nose, thinking, and he stifled a laugh at her overtly serious consideration. He had a feeling he shouldn't show his amusement, though, so he fought to keep a straight face while hoping she wasn't about to lasso him into an entire holiday break's worth of community service.

"Two shifts. And they have to be on a Saturday."

Whew. "Deal."

They shook hands, her palm still chilly in his. "Though I bet you'll want to volunteer more once you're there. It's contagious."

He'd take her word for it.

Preston gave her hand an extra squeeze before letting go. "I'll let you know the exact day and time of the dinner as soon as I confirm with my parents. In the meantime, we should probably meet up at least once beforehand to go over the things you'll need to know about me to be convincing."

Her eyes widened. "Wait. So this isn't going to be our first date?"

"Would *you* take a first date to a family Christmas dinner?"

"Point taken." She nodded briskly. "We should definitely practice, then, or it'll be obvious we barely know each other."

"Exactly." He pulled his cell from his pocket. "If you don't mind giving me your number, I can text you the specifics once I have them." He'd need to call his mom after this, not only to finalize the details, but to make sure she knew he had a date already secured. The last thing he needed was her showing up after their three-hour drive with a random woman in the back seat.

He and Lulu exchanged numbers, then she ducked out of his jacket and handed it to him. "Here you go. Thanks again."

He draped the coat over his arm. "Thank *you* for the donuts. And for the...arrangement." Such a formal word, but he didn't know what else to call it at this point.

Her eyes narrowed a little bit but before Lulu could reply, a custodian came around the corner, a white mop in tow. He looked surprised to see them. "You two are about to get locked in here."

Lulu thanked him, lifted one hand in an awkward wave to Preston, then made a beeline for the front door, as if being stuck with him was the worst possible outcome.

But it appeared in some ways she was already stuck. Hopefully she wouldn't regret it too much. He followed her to the parking lot at a slower place as he dialed his mom's number.

Hopefully neither of them would regret this.

Chapter Five

"Here comes the hill! Let's go!"

Lulu stood on her pedals, sweat dripping down her back as she joined Sandy and the rest of the class in their imaginary upward climb on the stationary bikes. Music pulsed through the room, a fast-paced, techno beat she didn't recognize.

Despite the rush of endorphins—and the constant burning in her quads—she couldn't stop thinking about last night's auction and her talk with Preston after. She hadn't expected—or even wanted—to be asked on a real date.

But she *really* hadn't expected to be asked on a fake one.

"Faster, ladies and gents. You can do it! Let's find some peaches to pick." Sandy, facing them from the front of the room under a cluster of mistletoe someone had hung over her bike station, was barely breaking a sweat. Neither was the fit woman in her seventies on the bike next to Lulu.

And yet, this was still easier than dating.

Lulu gasped for breath, trying to keep up with the rest of the class of regulars as her thoughts churned faster than her feet. Before Neal, she had loved her own quirky personality and had been proud of who she was. Proud of her gifts and passions.

She'd come a long way from her childhood riddled with poverty and insecurity, thanks to the Lord and a lot of encouraging truths learned in church.

But *after* Neal…well. She'd become hyper-aware of her awkwardness, her clumsiness, her inability to ever say the right thing at the right moment. Like everything she'd gotten okay with had suddenly become bad again. And being hyperaware just made her even *more* awkward and clumsy. It was a vicious cycle.

She wondered now if maybe she was too outside of the box to ever be considered dating material.

"Almost there! We'll pick those peaches at the top of the hill!"

Sucking in another tight breath as sweat dripped into her eyes, Lulu briefly imagined throwing said peaches at Sandy. Then thoughts of Preston invaded again. Did he see the same things Neal had seen after his parents pointed them out? Is that why he hadn't asked her on a true date after bidding on her?

Would she ever be worthy of the real thing?

It felt weird to be disappointed over something she hadn't necessarily wanted. Which made her think maybe a part of her *had* wanted it, and she was lying to herself.

Her thoughts were more exhausting than the class.

Sandy eased back into a sitting position on her bike. "Adjust your knobs, now. Let's coast for a minute at the top."

Lulu eagerly decreased the resistance, then plopped down on the seat and immediately regretted the fact that she hadn't worn padded shorts. Which made her remember the dress she had worn last night, how a part of her had hoped Preston would compliment her on it. But like most men these days, he'd only complimented her baking ability. Maybe the "fun donut lady" was all she was destined to be.

Her stomach clenched. Surely she had more to offer than that?

"Great job, everyone. Let's start our descent." Sandy began pedaling again, slower this time.

Lulu followed suit, wishing there was a knob to control her train of thought as easily. The truth was she'd halfway wanted Preston to ask her out. And the truth was that he hadn't.

But she could help him out as a loyal customer, even as a friend. She liked having friends, and they seemed destined to at least be that. After the one nondate, they could go back to their usual dynamic. Her life was predictable, and while that brought a certain measure of *blah*, it also provided a stability she hadn't ever known growing up. She liked stability.

And Preston had *not* shown himself to be predictable so far, except for maybe his recurring Friday donut order.

"That's it, everyone! We did it!" Sandy nimbly freed her feet from the stirrup pedals and hopped down.

"You did great, honey." The elderly woman next to Lulu dabbed at her glistening face with a white towel, while Lulu's hair remained plastered to her scalp. "It gets easier."

Did it? Lulu fumbled with her pedal straps, then pulled her foot free, unable to decide whether her legs or her rear end hurt the most. As she worked to free her other foot, her balance wavered, and she hit the ground in a heap.

Scratch that. Her pride hurt the most.

She pushed herself to a sitting position, reaching to massage her lower back as she breathed a silent prayer of gratitude that no one had seen her fall...

"Lulu?" A masculine voice, laced with humor and incredulity, filled the suddenly silent room. Preston.

"You weren't at church Sunday."

Preston blinked, but Lulu's gaze didn't waver. That wasn't the first thing he expected to hear from her as she clamored to her feet, ignoring—or perhaps not seeing—the hand he extended to help. Actually, it was more like the *last* thing he expected to hear considering how she'd just half tumbled off her stationary bike. Plus he'd seen her last night at the auction, and she hadn't mentioned a word about it.

Her stare demanded a response, and he fumbled for one. "I was there, but I sat in the back."

And left early, but this wasn't the time to get into that. He hadn't fully processed his own reasons for slipping out before the end of the sermon, and doing so in the gym probably wasn't the best time to start.

"Sorry, that sounded judgmental. I only meant I missed you." Lulu's eyes widened and she shook her head. "I mean, I missed *seeing* you."

"I knew what you meant." He hid his chuckle as he shifted his duffel bag to his other shoulder. She was cute when she was flustered, which seemed like most of the time lately. "Are you okay?" He gestured to the bike, sidestepping out of the way of an elderly woman in purple leggings attempting to leave the spin room. "I was just leaving the weight room when I saw you through the doorway."

"These things can be pretty tricky." She patted the seat of the bike she'd abandoned. "Ever tried spin class?"

"The weight bench is more my speed."

"These actually have multiple speeds."

He started to clarify what he'd meant, then realized she was joking. "Nice."

"It's not a pun, but..." She shrugged, her cheeks flushed and her hair sticking to her temples. On her, it was just cute. Gabrielle would never have been caught dead looking unkempt in public. In fact, the few times they'd worked out together at the gym back home, she'd worn a full face of makeup.

But why was he comparing them?

He gripped his bag strap tighter. "Listen, I was going to text you this afternoon. I talked to my mother and have the specifics for our..."

"Nondate?" Lulu supplied as she uncapped her water bottle.

That sounded bad. But not nearly as bad as *arrangement*, which was the word he'd used last night that seemed like it had suddenly shifted her mood toward him. He lowered his voice as the spin instructor clicked off the whirring fan in the front of the room. Was that mistletoe above her head? "I see this dinner more like a mission."

She nodded as she took a swig of water, her gaze following his to the holiday greenery hanging from the ceiling. "How about Operation Mistletoe?"

He snorted. "That'll work." He liked the idea of being on a team with Lulu. If he had to go through with this dinner charade, at least it was with a friend—one with a great sense of humor.

He really did owe her for this.

She checked her watch, then quickly recapped her bottle. "I want to hear the details, but I'm late. Come with me and help?"

He hadn't even worked out yet, but a spontaneous outing sounded a lot more fun than the weight bench. Besides, he'd just admitted he owed her. "Come where?"

"Follow me." She beckoned him out of the studio, then came to a sudden halt in the middle of the hallway, so fast he nearly ran into her heels. "But not quite yet. I have to run into the women's locker room first."

He stepped back and hid his smile as she darted through the blue swinging door.

Twenty minutes later, instead of carrying a gym bag, Preston found himself toting three boxes of hot donuts fresh from Oopsy Daisy onto the jobsite for the Haven Project.

"Yo, Teach!" Claudia greeted them by running from the construction area to snatch a box from the top of his stack. Aiden and Tori followed close behind over a mound of dirt, Tori bundled in a puffy purple jacket that looked like it was dusted with white dog hairs. "What are you doing here?"

"Helping." He held up the boxes. "I'm the official pack mule, apparently."

"You made it!" Lulu's voice pitched with delight as she hugged Claudia and Tori. Then she tapped the remaining boxes of donuts and smiled at Aiden. "Take these to the crew for me, okay?"

The trio obliged and jogged back up the hill to the construction site—except Aiden, who lagged a little behind with his head ducked, the donut boxes carefully in grip.

"He seems off lately." Lulu planted her hands on her hips as she observed the teen boy. "Have you noticed if he seems more...subdued?"

"He seems the same as always in class." Preston shrugged. "But then again, most teenagers aren't ecstatic over world history, so hard to say." He knew he'd been having trouble focusing himself lately, what with the holidays right around the corner. The kids probably had it way worse.

"I'm sure you make class interesting." Lulu

pulled out her phone before he could reply and opened her calendar. "So what time and where will Operation Mistletoe go down?"

"My house, this next Friday night." Preston rattled off his address. "Six o'clock."

She typed the info into her calendar, then pulled up a note app. "That means we have less than a week to practice knowing each other. What's your favorite color?"

"Blue." Cliché, but true.

"Like, sky blue? Royal blue? Navy?"

"All of them?"

She flipped one hand dismissively. "We'll go with navy. It's easier to remember." She typed furiously on the app.

"You're dictating my favorite color to me now?" He tried to hide his grin. "You're a bossy girlfriend."

"Bossy, huh?" She pursed her lips but didn't comment further. "So… What do you think *my* favorite color is?" She looked up and tucked her hair behind her ears, waiting expectantly.

For some reason, he really wanted to get this right. He thought for a moment, squinting as he studied her. Unfortunately, the multicolored workout top she'd worn in the gym didn't give a lot of clues, and was currently hidden under a white ski jacket. Her water bottle had been green. But that didn't really fit Lulu.

Then he remembered her store logo and smiled. "Yellow."

Her eyebrows rose. "Nice work."

"We probably already know more about each other than we realize."

Lulu shaded her eyes from the midday sun as she looked up at him. "You think?"

"Sure. For example—you're great with teenagers."

Pink tinged her cheeks. "Thank you. So are you."

"And you know your way around a good pun."

"Again—same to you."

He shifted his weight, suddenly unsure what to do with his hands now that he wasn't holding a gym bag or box of donuts. Weird—he'd never had that problem before.

The sound of an electric drill, mixed with the chatter up the slight hill to the site, nearly drowned out her next words. "I assume you're brave, since you're a teacher. That's not an easy job."

She saw him that way? A rush of warmth filled his chest, like he'd just gulped a big sip of his favorite coffee. "Well, I know *you're* brave, because you started your own business. Not to mention you're willing to dine with complete strangers on a holiday just to help a friend."

Her eyes softened as she laughed a little. "Brave…or foolish. Time will tell."

He found he wanted to keep going...wanted to keep her million-watt smile going. She wasn't hard to compliment. "And, on top of that, you make a mean donut."

Her grin faltered, casting her face in sudden shadow. "You know what? I should probably get up there, make sure the kids remembered their hard hats."

Before he could figure out what had just happened, she was gone, climbing the hill to the work in progress and leaving him feeling even more empty-handed than before.

Chapter Six

The next few days were filled with holiday donut baking, hyper teenagers on a sugar rush who were more than a little eager for their school break, and Operation Mistletoe text messages with Preston that went like:

Preston: Favorite food?

Lulu: Maybe tacos. Definitely not donuts.

Preston: Mine is sushi.

Lulu: The gas station on the corner of Main and Elm has great sushi.

Preston: So does The Sushi Den in the next town over.

Lulu: But why drive that far when you can get it here?

Preston: Because I don't want to drive to the ER after.

Lulu: Favorite animal?

Preston: I like dogs.

Lulu: Me too. We have a great shelter on the outskirts of town. Paradise Paws.

Preston: That's the one that Tori's uncle owns, right?

Lulu: Hence why she's always covered in dog hair.

Preston: Are you allergic to anything?

Lulu: Donuts, I think. Eye roll emoji.

Preston: Wait. Why did you type "eye roll emoji"? Do you not know where the emojis are on your phone?

Lulu: I'm not really a big texter.

and…

Preston: Why are you available to do this, by the way?

Lulu: I don't follow.

Preston: Why are you free for a holiday dinner?

Lulu: Because you asked me and I put it on my calendar?

Preston: I'm trying to tactfully ask why you're single.

Lulu: …

Preston: Are you still there?

Lulu: Why are you single?

Preston: Been focusing on my career. The last girlfriend was back toward the end of college, and we…parted ways.

Lulu: I see. Well, I got dumped.

Preston: His loss, I'm sure.

Lulu: His parents thought I was too much. Or maybe not quite enough. One of those.

Preston: Nah, you're goldilocks.

Lulu: ?

Preston: Just right.

Conversations with him—both via text or and in person—were easy, and Lulu felt embarrassed now about her overreaction to his donut compliment last Saturday at the jobsite. He had been trying to be nice and it wasn't his fault she was so sensitive about only being good at one thing. How could he possibly know that?

At least she had *something* to contribute to the world, even if it wasn't all she wanted.

She tried to be grateful for that fact as she awkwardly shifted her weight from one ill-fitting high heel to the other while standing in Preston's dining room. Grateful that this wasn't a real date, but only a fake one, which meant that it didn't *really* matter whether anyone in his family liked her or not.

Still, that didn't stop the butterflies from swarming her stomach as a car door slammed outside. Thoughts of meeting Neal's parents for the first time—at a sushi restaurant, ironically— filled her mind and threatened to turn the fluttering butterflies into something more like angry bats. That hadn't gone well. But this was different. She had to keep remembering this time was different.

Preston's texted words also fluttered around, much more gently than the bats. *Goldilocks.* Even though he was just being a friend, it was nice to hear.

She'd tried to text her mom about her and Preston's holiday plan several times, but always deleted it before sending. The situation felt too convoluted to try to explain via texting, and their occasional, poor-connection video chat attempts weren't conducive to the full story, either.

Of course, those could just be her excuses because she knew her mother wouldn't approve of the deception and would have talked her out of it.

"They're here." Preston joined her near the window, a muscle clenching in his jaw.

She felt the urge to press her finger against it, to smooth the stressed crease, but quickly curled her fingers into fists at her sides. He was legitimately on edge. Yet she was making all of this about her, rather than focusing on helping him.

Determined to be the best girlfriend in the shortest relationship ever, Lulu tapped his forearm. "Hey."

His worried gaze dropped to meet hers.

"This'll be fine, don't worry." She reached up and adjusted the tucked collar of his dress shirt to lay flat along the neckline of his navy sweater. Then she flashed him a grin. *"Honey."*

The tightness in his jaw released, and she felt a thrill of victory.

"You're right, *dear*." He returned her smile, then took a deep breath as four people piled out of a small silver car and a black SUV. "Let's get this over with."

Lulu wiped her palms down her red tulle skirt, hoping she'd paired it well with low heels she never wore and a fitted black top. It seemed Christmas-y enough, and Preston had said she looked nice when she'd arrived fifteen minutes ago, but then he'd gotten distracted with smoothing all the cloth napkins at each table setting. She'd jumped in to help and she hadn't really worried further about her appearance.

Until *right* now, as a tall, willowy blonde with legs for miles extending beneath an elegant black pencil skirt strode up the front walk, her hand loosely tucked through the arm of an attractive man who looked a lot like Preston. A little shorter and more compact, and clean shaven to Preston's permanent five-o'clock shadow, but there was no denying the brotherhood.

A man who had to be Preston's dad walked behind the couple, shorter like Preston's brother but burly, his gray hair thick and peppered. A petite woman with brown hair and wearing an embroidered holiday sweater walked next to him, carrying a foil-wrapped platter. Preston's mother.

Lulu mentally ran through the list of names he had quizzed her on. Harold and Susie Green, parents. Jackson and Gabrielle, newlyweds— and the reason Preston had asked Lulu to pretend with him.

Preston's jaw was clenched again as he opened the front door. "Hey, everyone. Come on in."

Lulu hung back anxiously as his family paraded inside, smelling like a mix of blended colognes and whatever cinnamon-heavy dish Preston's mother carried. Hopefully the older woman would be impressed with Lulu's homemade green bean casserole, complete with a secret ingredient.

But wait. It didn't *really* matter. She was already forgetting.

Mrs. Green set her sweet-smelling platter on the entry table and hugged Preston, and Lulu noted his tension eased while in her embrace. He truly cared about his mother, despite being tired of her matchmaking attempts.

"Hey, Mom."

"You look good, son. It's been too long." She cupped his face before scooping her side dish back up. Then she patted Lulu on the arm as she passed her and headed for the kitchen. "I'll just pop this in the oven. It's nice to meet you, dear. I can't wait to hear more about you!"

Lulu opened her mouth to reply, but Mrs.

Green was already breezing around the corner. Lulu swallowed. Probably for the best. In fact, the less she had to talk this entire evening, the better.

One down.

She nodded awkwardly at Mr. Green as he finished shaking Preston's hand and turned toward her.

"Well! You must be this Lulu I've been hearing about."

She flexed her fingers. "Yes, sir, I'm—"

Her next words were practically shoved back in her throat as she found herself swept into a big hug, her face smushed against the shoulder of Mr. Green's burgundy sweater. "I'm a hugger!" His voice boomed with energy and was so unlike Preston's more reserved ways, she couldn't help but smile.

Lulu hadn't had a hug from a father-type figure in…well, maybe for as long as she could remember. Neal's father certainly had never tried.

But it was silly to care. She was here for one evening, and one evening only. No sense in getting attached, even if Preston's parents were a lot nicer than she'd expected. "It's nice to meet you, Mr. Green." She meant it.

"It's Harold," he insisted. "None of this Mr. Green stuff. That's Preston's grandfather. And you might as well adapt to Susie instead of Mrs.

Green, too." He shot Lulu a wink as he continued farther into the house.

Two down.

She squared her shoulders as Jackson came through the line next, clapping Preston on the shoulder and then giving Lulu a half bow, half dip of the head. "Nice to meet you. I'm Jackson. And this is my wife—"

"Your place is just adorable, Pres," Gabrielle interjected, practically cooing as she tossed back her silky blond hair, which had somehow managed to hold salon-worthy curls even while traveling. A feat Lulu had never managed when she had longer hair. The willowy woman let her gaze flit over the cozy cottage before focusing back on Preston. She pointed at him with a long, French-manicured nail. "Did it come furnished?"

He nodded, looking sheepish as he shoved his hands in his slacks pockets. "Mostly."

"That explains it." Even her laugh was feminine, dainty and elegant. "I should have known."

Gabrielle and Preston had a familiarity Lulu hadn't expected, seeing how Preston had barely mentioned her in their Operation Mistletoe prep sessions. But it was good that they got along since he and his brother didn't. Maybe it would make the dinner less awkward for everyone.

The oven beeped from the kitchen as Mrs. Green—*Susie*, she corrected herself—heated up her side dish. Gabrielle and Jackson had followed Preston's parents, leaving Lulu alone with Preston briefly in the foyer.

"That wasn't so bad," she whispered.

"I suppose." Preston looked pained as he fidgeted with the neck of his shirt in the foyer mirror. "But it's only been forty-five seconds."

"Well, Gabrielle seems nice. Maybe you can count on her."

Preston coughed, hard, then nodded as his face flushed red. "Maybe."

"You keep doing that." As he coughed a second time, Lulu grabbed his arm and lifted it, surprised at how heavy his arm felt. He might have skipped his workout to help her last Saturday, but that was apparently the only time.

"And I keep telling you that whole arm trick doesn't stop a cough." Preston lowered his arm, and her hand, which was still resting on his sweater sleeve, slid down and brushed against his palm.

She quickly yanked her hand back. "Sorry."

"Actually, about that…" Preston stepped closer, lowering his voice. His cologne, which smelled a dozen times better than his brother's, wafted toward her, like a forest beckoning a woodland creature. "We never discussed…you know. PDA."

"PDA?" She hadn't meant to repeat that word

so loud and tried to whisper it instead. But it still escaped at top volume.

Preston gently pressed his finger against her lips, chuckling as he shot a look over his shoulder toward the kitchen—which was thankfully out of sight. He lowered his hand. "If we've been dating for months, they might expect us to hold hands at dinner. Or, you know, have my arm around you at some point."

"Oh. Right." Lulu cleared her throat. "Well… as you wish." Her heart thundered in her ears. They were just pretending, and it wasn't like he expected her to kiss him or anything.

Worry pinched his brow. "But I don't want you to do anything you're not comfortable doing."

"Why not just escort me to the table for now? Then we'll go from there." She tucked her hand into the crook of his arm, like she'd seen Gabrielle do with Jackson. She fought the urge to tighten her grip. Yep, Preston definitely hadn't missed any workouts.

"Come on, now, you two lovebirds." Susie popped her head around the hallway corner and winked at them. "Your father is getting hungry." Then she was gone as quickly as she'd appeared.

"Ready?" Preston smiled down at Lulu, and she noted *he* didn't appear fazed, which only made her feel more flustered.

But she couldn't let him know that.

"You heard your mother." Lulu swallowed, adjusting her grip on his arm. "It's showtime... *dear.*"

"Pass the sweet potatoes, please." Jackson pointed to the oversize platter next to his mother, who eagerly passed the dish she'd brought and then offered him the rolls, too.

They'd been eating for all of fifteen minutes, but Lulu could already see that Susie loved doting on her boys. She alternated between peppering Lulu with questions, shooting knowing glances between her and Preston and refilling Jackson's plate as they talked about his recent construction business expansion into Nebraska.

Gabrielle, however, in contrast to Jackson's eager consumption of everything in reach, daintily speared green beans from Lulu's special casserole one at a time, while keeping up steady chitchat with Preston, who still didn't seem like he'd regained his typical coloring. A permanent red flush hovered around his jawline... In fact, it seemed to only be increasing. Was he still that on edge?

"So tell me—what do you do, Lulu?" Harold asked, his voice still loud even though she could tell he had attempted to lower it and keep the conversation between the two of them. It didn't work. Silence fell across the table, and she sucked in a tight breath.

"I...bake." She stumbled over the best way to explain her choice of living.

"Bake...what?" Gabrielle questioned, another bean resting on her fork. How many had she actually eaten? At least Susie seemed to like Lulu's offering—and Preston, too. He'd eaten a good-size portion.

"Lulu owns her own donut shop," Preston supplied, edging his water glass away from his plate. His face was definitely flushed—now creeping up into his cheeks. What would his parents think of her profession? Would they expect something grander for their intelligent-teacher son?

It doesn't matter, she reminded herself. And that freedom gave her courage. Whereas with Neal's parents, her future had been on the hook, now, with Preston's, it was simple conversation, carrying on the temporary holiday facade they'd created.

"Oopsy Daisy Donuts." She waited for the censored expressions like her former fiancé's parents had worn to parade across their faces, but the expressions never came.

In fact, Susie beamed at her as she dug her fork into her salad. "That sounds so adorable. I bet it's precious."

Gabrielle offered a quick nod of approval.

"Such a fun name for this charming town! I'll have to try one of your donuts sometime."

"Well, how 'bout that." Harold patted his stomach. "Sign me up for a dozen."

A rush of warmth spread through Lulu's chest. They all looked like they meant the encouragement.

"Lulu makes the best donuts I've ever had." Preston swiped the last bite of the green bean casserole onto his fork, as if proving his statement about her cooking ability. "She creates all kinds of gourmet flavors, too. High-quality."

She should take his hand.

Lulu squirmed in her seat, unsure if she was brave enough to be that bold. But if this was really her boyfriend praising her self-made business and her baking skills, it was a natural segue into affection. Wasn't that what a girlfriend would do right now?

Before she could talk herself out of it, she took Preston's hand in hers.

And fought the urge to wipe her palm on her napkin.

His hand was so clammy, it made her own nerves look like child's play. Was he that nervous about the dinner? It seemed to be going decently. She peeked at him from the corner of her eye and noticed the red had crept around to his left ear—the one closest to her. She squinted.

Then she gasped, jerking back and dropping his hand. "Preston. Your ear!"

It was swelling, already noticeably larger than it had been a few minutes ago, and so red, it could be driving Santa's sleigh.

"Oh, son." Susie's eyes widened. "I think you're having a reaction."

Harold slammed one hand on the table. "Well, obviously, Susie. Someone get this boy some antihistamine."

Allergies? He hadn't ever mentioned… "Allergic to what?" Lulu asked. But her question was drowned out in the din of sudden commotion.

"It can't be that bad." Preston grabbed his spoon and held it up, trying to catch his reflection. Then he grimaced. "Whoa!"

Now the other ear was starting to swell, along with his lower lip.

Lulu shoved her chair back. Somebody had to do something!

"Where do you keep your medications?" Susie was already bustling toward the kitchen, tossing the question over her shoulder.

"Over the stove," Preston answered, still staring into his spoon with horror.

"I'll help!" Gabrielle chased after her before Lulu could decide if she was supposed to instead.

Across the table, Jackson held up his cell and

snapped a pic. "Too bad it's Christmas, not Halloween. You'd be a prize winner, big brother."

"Very funny." Preston's speech was starting to slur from his oversize lip, and he stood, then wobbled slightly.

Lulu grabbed his arm, her heart racing. "Let's go to the kitchen."

But then Susie reappeared, a basket full of tissue boxes, various over-the-counter medicine bottles and several bags of cough drops in hand. "I've got it." She pawed through the collection, presumably in search of Benadryl. "Hopefully you have some here."

"Preston." Lulu gripped his arm, partly for his benefit to stay upright and partly for hers. "What is going on?" Her heart thundered as she watched the puffiness in his face continue up toward his eyes.

"I have no idea. Nothing here had mushrooms in it." Preston shrugged before defeatedly dropping back into his chair. "I'm always so careful."

"Mushrooms?" Lulu's eyes widened. "You're allergic to mushrooms?"

Five pairs of eyes, one set considerably puffier than the rest, turned toward her. She licked her lips, unsure whom to look back at. The decorative clock on the wall of the dining room ticked a steady, torturous rhythm.

Finally, Gabrielle spoke. "You didn't know

that?" She probably didn't mean the disdain in her voice, but it was there all the same.

And she was right. Lulu should have known.

If she was Preston's girlfriend.

She swallowed, her gaze darting between all of them before finally landing on Preston's flushed and swollen face. Her confession burned on her tongue, and she wished there was a way to avoid it. But it was inevitable. "The secret ingredient in my green bean casserole is pureed garlic mushroom sauce."

"Oh, man." Preston began to help his mom paw through the basket.

Gabrielle's smoky eyes narrowed a bit with confusion. "He's been allergic to mushrooms his whole life. I can't believe that never came up."

In a real relationship, it would have. For someone who had been fake dating for two hours, it probably wouldn't have. Lulu fought the audible groan begging for escape. How was she going to get out of this? It wasn't even an odd allergy— mushrooms were a really common food. She had no excuse.

"Here it is!" Susie found the telltale pink bottle and quickly removed the lid. She began hunting for a measuring cup, but Preston grabbed the container from her hand and began to chug straight from the bottle.

Lulu racked her brain. Hadn't she and Preston talked about allergies in their text prep?

She tried to remember the exact conversation. Then her stomach twisted. Of course. He had asked about her allergies, but because of her donut joke, and the way the convo had turned to emojis and texting, he never followed through with his own admission.

She'd just poisoned her boyfriend.

Chapter Seven

"Well, now." Mom cradled her steaming mug of coffee as she settled into the end of the sofa next to Jackson and Gabrielle. "That was some excitement."

That was one way to put it.

Preston took another sip of his allergy medicine from his spot on the adjoining love seat, unsure if he was more concerned about potential anaphylactic shock or how ridiculous he must look to Lulu. She'd been incredibly quiet since dinner, which had ended rather abruptly, and now she kept making excuses to go back and forth to the kitchen, bringing everyone coffee and offering to cut more pieces of cheesecake for dessert.

Gabrielle leaned forward from the couch, her legs crossed as she held Jackson's hand. "Are you feeling better?"

She seemed genuinely concerned, which, of course, she would be. She was a nice woman, always had been—she'd felt terrible when she first started dating Jackson. At least she'd waited a few months after breaking up with Preston, but he had always had the sneaking sensation it was just a technicality. They obviously wanted it to look like she hadn't dumped him for Jackson, but the evidence pointed to the contrary. Preston had never been a big believer in coincidence.

He almost forgot she'd asked a question. He reached up and touched his ear, which seemed to be almost back to a normal size. The puffiness in his eyes felt as if it were receding, too. "A little better."

Nothing about tonight so far had gone as planned, but at least everyone seemed to be buying the fact that he and Lulu were together— despite their glaring oversight. He should have told her he was allergic to mushrooms. In fact, he couldn't believe he hadn't. He told everyone about his allergy before having a meal with them, but he'd been so focused on the charade, it'd never crossed his mind. And since Lulu was unlikely to ever bake donuts with mushrooms, he'd never felt a reason to mention it to her at her shop.

Lulu appeared in the living room doorway again, finally out of jobs to fill. He scooted over a little on the love seat and gestured for her to join him. She shook her head, and he motioned again, hoping no one was watching the brief exchange. Finally, the ruse and their expected roles must have registered because she quickly skirted the coffee table and joined him.

He considered taking her hand for appearance's sake, then realized he didn't want to put on an act. He just wanted to genuinely ask if she was okay. Wanted to assure her none of this was her fault, that she couldn't have possibly known. But his dad interrupted before he could whisper any of that.

"We know one thing, now, Lulu." The leather recliner across the living room creaked as his father rocked it slightly back and forth. "That green bean casserole was to die for!"

Jackson groaned. "Dad, come on."

Lulu covered her mouth with her hand before peeking up at Preston. "I'm really sorry."

"Come on, now. Let's not make the poor girl feel worse." His mother saluted Lulu with her coffee mug. "You'll have to get a thick skin with this bunch, sweetie."

Some of them more than others. Preston glanced at his brother.

"Moving on," Mom continued. "I have some good news to share."

"What's that?" Jackson asked as he looked up from his cell. "Do I already know?"

The fact he assumed he would have the inside scoop grated on Preston's nerves. His parents had never intentionally played favorites, but... Some things didn't have to be spoken. He quickly took the last sip of Benadryl to avoid starting an argument.

"We're going to stay here for the holidays!"

He almost sprayed pink liquid all over him and Lulu.

Preston gulped, coughed and shot Lulu a look that hopefully read *don't you dare lift my arm.* "Here?"

"Not here-here." Mom waved her free hand to indicate the living room. "In Tulip Mound. We'll get a B&B or a hotel...whatever you have."

What he had was a headache—one growing directly in proportion to his mother's announcement. He narrowed his eyes. "For how long, exactly?"

Lulu suddenly gripped his hand, and he realized how rude his tone sounded. He cleared his throat and tried again at a higher decibel. "For how long?"

But as usual, his question was lost in the throes of everyone else talking—everyone else deciding his life. Ironically, the exact thing he'd tried to avoid by bringing Lulu into this circus.

Except this time, it wasn't planning his love life but rather planning his holiday. His time off… all without his own input.

"That'll be wonderful." Gabrielle reached over Jackson to pat his mother's arm. "I'm sure Preston will love showing you around his new home."

He would?

"Oh, so *that's* why you wanted to take two cars on the drive over." Jackson nodded. "Makes sense now."

"Isn't there a Christmas tree farm around here?" Gabrielle gestured over her shoulder toward the front yard. "I saw a sign on our way into town."

"There *is*!" Mom exclaimed. "And they have reindeer there. Real reindeer."

"Sounds like you live in a snow globe, bro." Jackson grinned.

He certainly felt shaken up at the moment. Preston opened his mouth to speak, but before he could, Dad set his dessert plate on the end table with a clink of his fork against glass. "The trunk's loaded up with suitcases and we plan to get to know your town, son."

Suitcases. Plural.

"That's…great." Preston briefly closed his eyes, wondering if the medicine was kicking in and causing the nausea or if it was solely due to the conversation circling around him.

"I just couldn't stand the thought of you being here all alone for Christmas, and I knew you wouldn't come stay with us for long. Now we can spend your holiday break with you." Mom smiled widely pulling Lulu into her declaration. "With *both* of you."

Lulu's wide-eyed stare up at him looked as panicked as he felt. And then he realized the most obvious problem of all. There was no way they could continue this fake dating for more than the one night. Asking a new friend to be a date for Christmas dinner was one thing, but living a lie for two weeks? Impossible.

This had to stop.

"You have to tell them," Lulu whispered, her brown eyes drawing him in.

"I know," he whispered back. But they'd moved on to talking about other festive events they could hit up while in town. He was pretty sure he just heard the words *snowman contest*.

"Now." Lulu tugged his hand with urgency.

She was right. No sense in procrastinating. He took a deep breath, regret filling his chest. They shouldn't have done this. He was going to look like a fool, but he'd brought it on himself. "Listen, guys, there's something you should—"

"Just a moment, son. While we're on announcements." His father cleared his throat, then shot his mom a meaningful glance. "There's one more."

They were moving to Tulip Mound permanently? Jackson and Gabrielle were expecting a baby?

He wasn't sure which would be the harder of the two to hear.

"Oh, Harold, are you sure?" Worry flooded Mom's face.

Preston's stomach knotted and his heart sank. He knew that look. He'd seen it almost daily for six months back when—

"I'm afraid my cancer is back."

The room tilted. Forget snow globe… This felt more like a mirrored fun house in a carnival. Nothing was as it appeared.

"Dad." The knot leaped from Preston's stomach to his throat, and it wasn't the lingering remains of the allergy closing off his breath. Lulu gripped his hand again, this time in support instead of conviction. He clung to it as his vision narrowed.

Across the room, Jackson went pale, and Preston couldn't even muster any relief that his brother clearly hadn't known this news first. Next to him, Gabrielle rubbed Jackson's knee, her typically arched brows dipped with concern.

"Now, don't worry." His father held up both hands, his gaze landing on each of them. "They caught it early, like last time. The prognosis is good."

"Very good," Mom confirmed. Her voice radiated a confidence that her shaking coffee cup belied. She must have noticed too because she quickly handed the mug off to Jackson. "He's already had one round of chemo. His next will begin immediately after Christmas."

That was why they'd wanted to come.

And why they wanted to stay.

He swallowed. How could he tell them now? He shot a glance at Lulu, who somehow seemed to understand his internal dilemma. But all she offered was a slight shrug as she rolled in her lower lip.

He'd have to wait…maybe catch his parents alone later in the evening. No way could he drop that truth bomb right in the aftermath of his dad's grenade. And preferably not in front of Jackson.

Still holding Lulu's hand—and not because anyone expected him to—he angled toward his father. "Are you feeling okay? Do you need anything?" He should have noticed. In hindsight, it seemed obvious something was going on—his dad was a few pounds lighter. His hug hadn't been quite as strong. And he hadn't eaten hardly anything sweet.

All like last time.

"I feel fine. Wishing there was more of that green bean casserole." He grinned at Lulu, who immediately blushed. Then his tone sobered a bit. "I'm sure that'll all change with the additional chemo, but we'll deal with it."

"Exactly." Mom took the hand Jackson offered, her voice forcibly upbeat. "As a family. With the Lord, we'll get through this a second time...with bells on." She winked, her eyes slightly glassy.

"Look, I'm not usually the sappy type, you all know that." Dad nodded at Lulu. "Or at least, you will. But I have to say, after getting that news from the doctor last week... It does me good to see my boys settled with two good women." His voice cracked.

The room fell silent.

Preston's heart thudded. Forget telling his parents the truth later that evening.

How could he tell them *at all*?

Lulu stared into the sink full of dishes, suds coating her arms halfway to her pushed-up sleeves, and wondered what it would take to recover from this evening. Apparently now she couldn't even *pretend* to date without some catastrophe.

What were they going to do?

She rinsed a salad plate and set it on the drying rack to the left of the sink, catching her reflection in the kitchen window overlooking the front yard. She looked as tired as she felt, her carefully styled hair limp and lifeless. The quiet stillness of the dark evening beyond her gaze belied the chaos that had occurred just a half hour ago. After Preston's allergic reaction and his parents' two announcements, she eagerly insisted on doing dishes, giving his family a much-needed moment alone.

This was a family in crisis, and she was in the way—yet stuck, all at the same time. Even before Mr. Green's—*Harold's*—grim news, Lulu hadn't known what to do. But Gabrielle did. She was an excellent wife and daughter-in-law, consoling Susie, dropping everything to aid Preston during the mushroom fiasco...even knowing he was allergic in the first place. Lulu sighed.

She didn't belong here.

Preston's reflection suddenly appeared in the window beside her, and she jumped, flicking suds onto the counter.

"I can't have my girlfriend doing dishes without me." His tone hinted he was as exhausted as she felt, despite the small smile he wore.

She scrubbed at a stain on her casserole pan, avoiding his gaze. "It's no problem. I thought your family might need some privacy."

"I figured." He picked up a kitchen towel and motioned for the next dish. "Thanks for helping."

"It's the least I could do after I almost killed

you." Lulu handed him a dessert plate, then finally looked up, giving him a quick once-over. "You look normal now."

"Well, if by normal you mean *dashingly handsome*, I'll take it."

Lulu snorted. "What do you think this is, a Hallmark movie?" Her heart fluttered like it could be, and she quickly stuffed the nonsensical feeling aside. She'd ridden a roller coaster of emotions in the past hour—no need to make it anything more than it was.

Even if Preston did look *dashingly handsome* with his shirtsleeves rolled up and his collar unbuttoned.

"Feels a little like a holiday movie." Preston dried the plate, then stacked it atop the last one. He leaned one hip against the counter and ticked off points on his finger. "The fake date, the medical emergency, the surprise announcement from a family member..." Then his smirk faded, and he sobered. "But unfortunately, this is all too real."

It was. And she was being selfish again, letting her insecurities take center stage when Preston was the one going through the sudden trial. She was his friend, wasn't she? She should do whatever she could to help—and dishes didn't count.

She spun toward him, barely remembering to

keep her dripping hands hovering over the sink. "What do you want to do? About…you know. Us."

He cast a glance over his shoulder toward the French doors separating the living room from the kitchen. "I wanted to come clean. It felt right. But now…" His voice trailed off and he shrugged. His blue gaze anxiously searched hers as if seeking permission for something.

She didn't know what and was a little afraid to ask. Also a little afraid of all the impulses nudging her to hug Preston. But she resisted. After all, no one was around for them to keep up the charade right now.

Yet she didn't want to pretend—she wanted to reassure a friend who had just gotten bad news.

"But now?" She urged him to continue as she went back to scrubbing a drinking glass, keeping her hands very much to herself.

"Now… I don't know. Last time, Dad really struggled with his blood pressure during chemo. He gets stressed out easily anyway, and when his body was weaker from the treatments, his stress got worse and affected his vitals. His doctor told us it was important to help keep his anxiety down." Preston ran one hand through his dark hair, the weight of the new burden evident in the hunch of his shoulders. "Now I'm afraid that if I tell him the truth, he'll be so disappointed, he'll carry that stress right into his treatments."

His voice cracked, and Lulu couldn't take it anymore. She flung her wet arms around him in a hug and squeezed tight.

He stiffened, then wrapped his arms around her, too, and pressed his cheek against the top of her head.

"I'm sorry you're all having to go through this again," she muttered into his shoulder, aware that her hands were leaving damp imprints on his button-up shirt. He'd ditched the sweater earlier during his allergy attack, claiming to be hot, and now, she could feel the athletic firmness of his back.

"I'm sorry I've pulled you into this," he whispered against the top of her hair.

His nearness sent a warm shiver down her spine. Could he feel her heart thundering out of her chest? She pulled back, but he only let go enough for him to meet her eyes.

His voice deepened. "You can get out if you want to."

Of their deal, or his embrace? She hesitated, soaking in his steady gaze. And she realized with a strange mixture of horror and anticipation—she didn't want to get out of either.

Where, oh where, was a spin class when she needed one?

Lulu swallowed, not breaking eye contact. "If you think it's for the best, then I want to help." Preston's arms, still loosely wrapped around her, felt like a safe haven. "We can keep up the charade a little longer—for your dad's sake."

"You don't have to, you know." Preston's Adam's apple bobbed in his throat. "You didn't sign up for this."

She squeezed his arm, where her hands rested near his elbows. "Neither did you."

"No hard feelings if you want to bail." He raised his eyebrows, which were slightly puffier than usual from his allergic reaction. "Are you sure?"

Was she? Her rapid heartbeat ticked off the seconds as she held his gaze. She liked Harold—she didn't want to trick him. But she liked him enough to do what was best. And if Preston believed keeping his father's stress low through the holidays was best, then she would do whatever it took to help. Hopefully, they'd have plenty of opportunity for the truth when it wouldn't carry such a bite.

This man in front of her was a good man who was trying to be a good son. How could she not support that? She'd never had a father long enough to imagine what she'd do if the situation was reversed. But she *could* imagine how much it would mean to have a father fight for her well-being, and that thought sealed the deal.

"I'm sure." Her whispered words hovered between them.

Relief flooded Preston's face, then a ghost of a smile lifted his lips. "Operation Mistletoe—Phase Two."

The kitchen doors suddenly cracked open. Preston and Lulu jumped apart, soap bubbles dripping onto the floor as Susie strolled inside.

She stopped short when she saw them, then smiled. "You two lovebirds. Though I suppose in honor of the season, I should say *turtledoves*." She winked. "Don't mind me." She took her purse off the barstool and pushed back through the doors.

Lulu quickly busied herself with the dishes again, her heart sinking. That was the whole problem.

She was starting not to mind any of this at all.

Chapter Eight

The past few days had been so full of unexpected events, Preston almost didn't bat an eye when his mom suggested they all visit the Christmas tree farm on the outskirts of town—the one featuring live reindeer. After a fake girlfriend and his father's health news, the idea seemed right in line with all that had been happening.

He eyed his parents, walking hand in hand a few steps ahead of him and Lulu, and took a deep breath.

"Have you been here yet?" Lulu asked as she wrapped a thick yellow scarf around her neck. The snow that had fallen the previous night crunched under their feet as they made their way up the hill from the parking lot to the Rockin' Reindeer Ranch sprawled before them. A giant pair of iron Rs, one turned backward and interlaced with the other, decorated a wooden sign high above their heads.

Somewhere in the near distance, a reindeer grunted. He could relate. At least Jackson and Gabrielle had decided to stay back at the hotel today instead of joining them, thanks to a work emergency Jackson had to handle, or Preston's internal grunts would be more like groans. His brother and his blushing bride would be heading home tomorrow after their planned family dinner out that evening. One more quick meal, then he could go back to not seeing his brother for several months.

His parents, however, would remain at the Hummingbird Inn for the next week-plus at a discounted rate, thanks to the generosity of the manager, Noah Montgomery, who claimed that "any family member of a new Tulip Mound resident was family of theirs."

Guilt tapped Preston on the shoulder. Now not only was he tricking his parents—even if it was for their own good—he was getting discounts for a residency he wasn't intending to keep. As charming as Tulip Mound seemed, he had no intention of making it his permanent home. He had goals of becoming a professor, of becoming someone who *mattered*, and that couldn't be accomplished in this tiny town in Kansas.

Then he realized someone was actually tapping his shoulder. Lulu.

He glanced down at her, her cheeks red from cold. "I'm sorry. Did you say something?"

"I asked if you'd been here before. Since moving to Tulip Mound." Lulu motioned at the ranch before them, where kids giggled as they posed next to a tall cardboard Christmas sleigh, their own faces serving as the face of the deer.

He shook his head. "Can't say that I have." As festive as the Rockin' Reindeer was—a combination snack shop, Christmas tree farm and working ranch with a reindeer petting zoo—he couldn't quite get in the holiday spirit. He was distracted about his dad, but on top of that, Preston felt himself holding back.

This wasn't going to be his home for very long.

A jingling of bells sounded from a nearby paddock like an off-key Christmas choir, and his mother squealed with delight. She hurried to the fence, removing her glove before reaching over to pet the dark brown head of one of the deer. "These guys are so cute. Aren't they cute, Harold?"

Dad shoved his hands in his pants pockets, clearly indicating he wasn't about to touch the animal. "Absolutely adorable, dear."

"I wish Jackson and Gabrielle could see this." Mom frowned. "I hate that they're missing it."

Preston sighed. His mom was doing that thing she did last time Dad was sick—attempting to wring every single ounce of fun she could from every experience, and then make sure he was doing the same. It was a little awkward, but more than that, it reminded Preston of the grim reality they were all navigating.

This Christmas could be his father's last.

"Come on." Lulu suddenly tucked her gloved hand through the crook of Preston's elbow and tugged him toward the main cabin, which was laced with real boughs of holly. "Let's go get a snack."

"What about them?" Preston nodded toward his parents as he stumbled after her.

"I think they'll be fine." She grinned as his mother posed for another reindeer selfie. "We'll bring them back some chestnuts."

Inside the snack shop it was much quieter, as the snow-suited children and their camera-snapping parents were all still outside. The aroma of cinnamon and sugar hit hard, igniting Preston's taste buds, then was followed by the hickory scent of coffee. He immediately relaxed, rolling his shoulders down and back and releasing a tight breath he hadn't realized he'd been holding.

"Better?" Lulu slipped her hand from his arm. Of course. They were no longer under a pretense.

He missed her calming touch, though, but that fact was only further evidence of his anxiety. She was a soothing presence, that was all. He appreciated her consideration. Gabrielle had never noticed things like that when they dated. "How did you know I needed a minute?"

"You just sort of looked stressed." She shrugged as she stepped up to the counter decorated with twinkle lights and paper snowflakes. "Black coffee, I'm assuming?"

He nodded, a little surprised but also relieved as she efficiently secured them two coffees and two bags of roasted chestnuts, tied with curly red ribbon.

The middle-aged barista wearing a forest green apron smiled at them as she shut the register. "You might be interested in the back patio." She nodded toward a balcony to the back of the shop and gave a knowing smile.

Of course, she couldn't know that they weren't really lovebirds...*turtledoves*, as his mother called them...seeking a private moment. But he'd take the quiet for as long as he could.

They settled at a wrought iron table for two on the balcony, which overlooked the other side of the snow-dusted hill, and sipped their drinks. The acreage sprawled for miles, open pasture giving way to rows and rows of fully grown Christmas trees. Kids in brightly colored jackets darted between the rows. Reindeer called from the paddocks below.

The knot that had taken permanent residence in his stomach unraveled a tad. Maybe he could start to ease into the holiday mood after all. Then a sudden thought intruded.

"Let me reimburse you for all this." Preston quickly reached for his wallet, guilt nudging him again for the oversight, but Lulu shook her head, pressing his hand away.

"I've got it. Don't worry." Then she promptly knocked over her coffee cup. "Oops."

He stood. "I'll grab some napkins."

"My mess. I've got it." Lulu rolled her eyes. "I'm used to it, trust me."

He settled back in his chair as she rushed away, the knot back and tighter than ever. He felt helpless. About his father's health, about navigating this charade with Lulu. And now helpless to even stop the river of coffee currently running off the side of the table and onto the wooden planks.

He wanted to pray, but the words felt dry. Sort of like his Christmas spirit. How had everything changed so quickly? *Lord...* He couldn't get any further. Whatever had made him leave church early last Sunday was tying his thoughts up now, blocking his prayers from getting past the over-hanging roof of the Rockin' Reindeer balcony.

He'd felt that way for a while. His church attendance the last year had waned, or maybe his prayers had waned first. He wasn't sure. But all his recent efforts had been toward trying to achieve his ultimate goal of becoming a professor. *Then* he could relax, get his spirit settled and move forward in life. He would have finally arrived. Finally have a real status with which to prove himself to his family.

But this news about his dad had thrown a kink in his plan. Preston hadn't counted on needing the Lord so desperately before he had all his academic ducks in a row. No wonder he felt blocked when he tried to pray. Maybe God knew Preston had stopped making Him a priority, and it wasn't fair to come back now when times were tough.

Lulu returned with a fistful of napkins and a fresh coffee. "She was sweet to give me another one. I tipped her."

"You're really generous." The compliment flew off his lips before he could figure out if it was appropriate.

Lulu sat quietly, blinking at him as she carefully held her cup with both hands.

Too late to backpedal now. Besides, just because they were in a fake relationship didn't mean he couldn't say real things.

"Not just for the tip." He set his coffee down on the table but kept his fingers laced around it for the warmth. "You're generous in spirit. You noticed I needed to get away for a minute and made it happen. Even bought the snacks."

"You've been through a lot in the last few days." Lulu lifted one jacket-clad shoulder in a shrug. "Like I said, it's the least I can do."

"You're going above and beyond, trust me."

"That's what friends are for. Right?" Her deep brown gaze searched his, and for a moment, he couldn't tell if she was asking for clarification of her basic statement…or seeking clarification that they were, indeed, friends.

"Right." He nodded firmly, hoping his answer would cover it either way. Of course they were friends. In fact, this whole fake-dating charade had only proved how much he did enjoy her friendship.

Watching her sip her coffee, her expression unreadable as she gazed out across the rows of trees, he decided to take one more risk. "I'm sorry this all got so complicated, but… I am glad I asked you to do this."

She set her cup down, reaching across the table to touch his forearm. "You know what? I am, too."

Then she accidentally knocked over his coffee.

* * *

Even though the snow only reached halfway up the soles of her boots, Lulu was in way over her head.

She kept her hand tucked in the curve of Preston's elbow as they ambled behind Harold and Susie through the sculpted rows of fir trees, mostly to keep her footing in the slippery mixture of snow and ice. Phase Two of Operation Mistletoe had officially begun. She couldn't decide which was more confusing—pretending to date Preston, or that she kept forgetting she was only pretending.

But Preston hadn't asked her to date him. In his eyes, she was simply a friend providing a favor. And if she'd learned anything during the whole fiasco with Neal and his parents, it was that she didn't want to be second best.

"This tree looks perfect." A few yards ahead, Susie stopped in front of a tall fir, craning her neck to see the top. "What do you think, Pres?"

"Pres?" Lulu tried to hide a snicker behind her glove as Preston's face flushed. "Like, President?"

Preston squinted at his mother. "Mom, may I remind you, I have a rental cottage in Tulip Mound. Not a mansion in Beverly Hills. There's no way that tree would fit in my living room."

Susie huffed. "I've never been good at gauging measurements."

"Do you know the difference between an inch and a mile? That might be a good starting place." Preston winked at Lulu, and she stifled another laugh. It was good to see him happy, good to see the weight of his new burden momentarily lifted.

Susie chuckled as she bumped her hip lightly into Lulu's. "See what I put up with?" She patted Lulu's shoulder. "I'm glad between you, me and Gabrielle, we finally even out the men!"

"Not if Lulu keeps trying to murder Preston with mushrooms." Now it was Harold's turn to laugh.

She opened her mouth to participate in the jesting, but a female voice suddenly lilted through the trees.

"Guess who made it!"

They turned in time to see Jackson and Gabrielle trudging toward them, dragging a sled that carried a coil of thick rope, an ax and a saw. Gabrielle's hair was piled on top of her head in an intentionally messy topknot, and her cream-colored scarf and matching gloves were all elegance against her slim-fitting peacoat and boots.

"Jackson got everything squared away at work, so we decided to meet you guys." Gabrielle looped an arm around Susie's shoulders, her cheeks flushed prettily. She looked like she could be posing for an ski lodge advertisement.

Her heart shifted toward disappointment, and she couldn't immediately pinpoint why.

She glanced back at Preston and saw the happy air fading from his expression.

"Sorry you drug that out here for nothing." Preston nodded toward the sled. "We're going to pick the tree, then get the staff to cut it down for us."

"Why? Not afraid of a little hard work, are you?" Jackson asked, theatrically puffing out his chest.

A shadow flickered across Preston's face and Lulu felt a surge of protection. "Of course not." She stepped forward. "Preston is a hard worker."

"Of course." Gabrielle laid one hand on Jackson's shoulder and smiled. "They both are."

Lulu moved to Preston's side, matching the other woman's pose. "I think Preston was just trying to be considerate of the...*situation*."

She darted a pointed look toward Harold, who thankfully was staring up at the enormous fir Susie had chosen and seemed oblivious to the exchange. Obviously Preston didn't want his dad to exert himself by helping chop down their tree when the ranch offered both self-serve and staff-assisted options. Some things—like peace of mind for Harold's health—were worth paying extra for.

Understanding dawned as Gabrielle followed Lulu's gaze. "Right."

But Jackson didn't seem to take the hint. "If Preston doesn't want to do it, I will." He grabbed the ax from the sled and started toward the row of trees.

Preston stiffened under Lulu's touch, his eyes narrowed. "It's not that."

"Hey, babe." Gabrielle raised one hand toward her husband. "I don't think—"

"Which one?" Jackson questioned, looking toward the trees.

"Well, not that one." Susie gestured to the one above her. "Apparently it's too big."

"What about this one?" Jackson pointed with the ax to a similar, yet significantly shorter, fir farther down the row.

"Perfect!" Gabrielle clapped her gloved hands together.

Preston let out a slow breath. "Do I get a vote on my own tree?"

"I'll help." Harold uncuffed one shirtsleeve and began to roll it up.

"Don't you dare." Susie glowered.

Frustration tinged his face as he reluctantly rolled his sleeve back down.

Compassion tugged at Lulu's heart. It had to be maddening to be limited—especially if he was used to being the one to take care of his family.

Susie sighed as she relented. "You can help the boys put it on the sled." The second Harold turned his back to pick up the saw, Susie widened her eyes at both of her sons, indicating they better not let him bear the brunt of any of the work.

"Here, Dad. I've got it." Preston took the saw from his dad, his jaw clenched.

Lulu wasn't sure whom to console first—Harold or Preston. His family, while meaning well, tended to talk over him. No wonder he'd wanted her to fill in as a date. She could only imagine how stressful it would be to have all that familial energy focused directly on the topic of his love life.

"No, I've got it," Jackson interrupted as Preston moved into position beside the tree. "You said you didn't want to." He shoulder-bumped him out of the way, lowering the ax against the trunk. "Stand back and watch a real man work."

A muscle in Preston's cheek jumped. "Jackson, it's my tree. I'll do it." He held up the saw. "This works better, anyway."

Jackson snorted. "Fat chance."

Lulu swallowed. "Guys, maybe this isn't—"

Jackson swung the ax into the trunk. "See?"

But before he could get a second blow, Preston swooped in with the saw and began slicing through the bark.

"Dude." Jackson stepped back, the ax hanging at his side. "I said I've got it."

"Go get another tree, then."

"We only need one—for *my* house." Preston continued sawing. The second he took a break, Jackson swung the ax.

Saw.

Swing.

"Boys!" Harold barked. "Someone is going to get hurt."

Lulu darted her gaze between Jackson and Preston as they continued to fight over the tree. Harold grew paler and paler, and he reached out to steady himself on the trunk of a nearby spruce.

But no one noticed, as they continued to shout over each other and the cacophony of splitting wood. She had to do something.

Lulu put two fingers in her mouth and whistled. *"Hey!"*

Jackson stopped midswing. Preston stood abruptly, the saw dangling at his side.

Lulu cleared her throat. "Why are Christmas trees so bad at sewing?"

Everyone stared at her, then at each other, then back at her, as if this clumsy, mushroom-cooking intruder to their family had finally lost her remaining marbles.

But she didn't care. All she cared about was the color returning to Harold's face, and the subtle drooping of his shoulders as he relaxed. A small smile crept across his cheeks. He straightened, no longer holding the trunk for support. "Why's that, darlin'?"

She smiled back. "They keep dropping their needles."

Chapter Nine

Preston threaded a hook through the tiny hole on top of the ornament he held and stuck it deep inside a branch. Standing in front of the tree they'd brought home a few hours ago only made him relive the disastrous afternoon spent on the ranch, which made his regret steep stronger than the tea in his mother's abandoned mug. His parents had taken a break from decorating the tree to get Harold some fresh air on the patio, but he also figured they were trying to give him and Lulu "alone time."

Which he wanted, but not for the reason they'd assumed. The second the door had shut behind them a few moments ago, the need to blurt the truth had become nearly overwhelming. Plus, the way he'd behaved earlier was downright ridiculous, and very out of character for him.

For some reason he couldn't fully explore yet, it was important Lulu realize that.

"I'm an idiot," he declared.

She stepped back and studied the partially decorated fir, her expression calm as always. "Personally, I wouldn't have put that red ball so close to the other red one, but that doesn't mean you're an idiot."

He stifled a laugh. She *always* made him laugh. "I meant about what happened at the ranch. With Jackson."

"Ah. That." Lulu casually moved the ornament he'd just hung a few branches higher, as if maybe she'd hoped he wouldn't notice. "You're competitive. It happens."

"That wasn't just competition." Preston shook his head, unsure why he was throwing himself under the proverbial bus with this sudden confession but needing to confess all the same. "I was trying to show him up."

She adjusted a strand of garland draped across the tree. "Why?"

That was the big question. Partly because it was Jackson, and his brother always had to come out on top. Preston really wanted him to come in second place, just once. Jackson already had the favor, the girl, the lucrative career.

As for the other reason, well… "For you, partly."

She reached into the box for another ball. "You don't have to actually impress me, remember? As far as your family is concerned, you've already won me over." She wrinkled her nose. "Besides, I might be a little out of practice when it comes to real dating, but I don't think the whole 'who can beat on their chest and yell the loudest' approach really works on women anyway."

"Fair." He laughed as he hung another ornament. "So what does work?"

Lulu blinked at him, an angel figurine dangling from her fingers. "Why?"

"Just curious."

She moved the decoration he'd just hung to a branch lower. "Someone noticing things, I think. Little things."

"Like your favorite color."

She shot him a look then, one he couldn't read, and nodded slowly. "Like that."

"So being seen is romantic."

She kept her focus straight ahead, not meeting his eyes. "When you're usually only noticed for things you'd rather not be, it's nice to have the opposite now and then."

He tilted his head, studying her face by the glow of the twinkle lights. Lulu was one of a kind, no doubt about it. A little clumsy and awkward at times. Cute, but not necessarily what the world would call gorgeous. However, he found her to be the most genuine woman he'd ever met.

With Lulu, there was no pretense. No games. Everything was so real. Authentic.

Except, of course, their relationship.

He cleared his throat. "I suppose after all this chaos today, I owe you more Haven Project hours now."

"A few."

He kept noticing how the twinkle lights were shining in her eyes, so he tried to focus on threading another hook instead. "For the record, I am sorry for earlier, back at the ranch. I acted barbaric."

She took the ornament he'd prepared and hung it, a smile teasing her lips. "It *wasn't* that bad. At least you didn't turn your tree-cutting weapons on each other."

"Come on. It was so bad, you had to tell a bad pun to break us up." He picked up a gold ball and tucked it into the branches.

She snorted. "I'm glad I had a few ready."

"You're funny, you know." In the best way possible.

She rolled in her lower lip. "And I make a mean donut, right?" Then she quickly scooted the gold ball onto a different branch.

Before he could reply, the back door opened. Mom stepped into the living room, her cheeks flushed from the cold. "Dad wants some coffee, if you have any." Then she whispered, "Make sure it's decaf, okay?"

"I'll get it." Lulu shoved the next decoration at Preston's chest and hurried to the kitchen, where they'd brewed a fresh pot upon arriving home.

"This is looking nice." Mom crossed her arms, standing back to survey the tree like Lulu kept doing. Must be a woman thing.

He hung the next ornament, and Mom reached for it. "Maybe over here, instead."

Definitely a woman thing.

Lulu came back, a steaming mug in hand. "Be right back." Then she quickly stepped outside. Was she that eager to deliver the coffee—or escape their prior conversation?

Knowing Lulu and her love of helping, probably both. She kept doing that—escaping when their conversations ran a little deeper. Maybe she wasn't as comfortable around him yet as he'd assumed.

Mom excused herself to the bathroom, so Preston eased closer to the door separating the back patio from the living room, peering through the partially slanted blinds. Not exactly eavesdropping, just… Okay, maybe he was eavesdropping. But he wanted to know she was okay and not upset about the donut remark again.

"Thank you, my dear." Dad took the cup from

Lulu and gestured to the chair beside him that Mom had vacated. "Join me?"

Lulu hesitated only a moment before plopping onto the cushioned seat. She pulled her legs up under her and rested her chin on her knees, then murmured something Preston couldn't quite catch.

"I agree." Dad's hearty voice left no room for error. "I can see why Preston likes this place."

He did? Preston leaned closer to the door. I mean, yes, he was starting to like Tulip Mound. Lulu was helping with that. But this town was still just a means to an end. And after he and Lulu finished Operation Mistletoe, he wouldn't see her as much—which felt oddly disappointing. But he could visit her at Oopsy Daisy anytime he wanted. They would still be friends.

Funny how pretending to be more felt kind of nice, though.

They were talking again. Preston fiddled with an ornament—one his mom or Lulu would probably move later anyway—and strained to catch the rest of the conversation.

"You're good for him, you know." Dad's voice carried easily through the windowed wall.

Lulu's response was harder to hear. "…glad you think so."

"He hasn't dated anyone in a while." His fa-

ther chuckled. "Though I'm probably not supposed to tell you that."

Definitely not. Preston frowned as he stuck
the glittery ball he held onto the tree. If he and
Lulu had been really dating, that would have
been beyond awkward.

But they weren't. He had to keep remembering that.

Dad continued. "His mother always tried to
play Cupid with her friends' daughters, but that
never seemed to work out."

"…with being single?"

"Nothing wrong with being single, of course."
Dad paused as he took a sip of coffee. "But as
a parent, you hope to see your children happy
and settled. You want to know they'll be okay,
that they won't be alone. Especially if, well, you
know…you're in my particular situation."

His voice trailed off and Lulu reached over
and patted his shoulder. Preston couldn't hear her
murmured words, but watching Lulu comfort his
father spread warmth through his chest. She was
going over and above. She might be pretending
to date Preston for the holidays, but everything
about her showed genuine concern for his dad.

He eased away from the blinds, staring into
the tree lights until they blurred. Gabrielle had
always been great with his parents—she'd liked
them when they'd dated, and she liked them now,

of course, as official daughter-in-law. But he'd never seen her be so candid with his dad, so real and vulnerable. With Gabrielle, there was always a layer Preston couldn't quite get through. A pretense of perfection. There was nothing wrong with being proper and put together all the time, but there was something so refreshing about Lulu's *imperfections*. It made him feel safe.

Like he didn't have to be so perfect, either.

"I want to make you something. What kind of donuts do you…" Her voice cut out again as she leaned forward and tucked her hair behind her ears, her face lit with anticipation. She really seemed to enjoy giving. Of her time, her abilities—even in things she wasn't sure about, like being auctioned off for the date that landed her in this whole mess in the first place. Not to mention helping build an entire house for a good cause.

A twinge of guilt pricked his conscience. Lulu was continually sacrificing, yet here he was, eager to climb the career ladder and leave Tulip Mound and his students behind as fast as he'd arrived. Not to mention he'd refused to be part of the fundraising auction and had to be talked into volunteering at the Haven Project.

Maybe Lulu *was* kind of perfect, in the ways that truly mattered.

"I'm afraid here lately sweet things don't taste

very good. But I'd be happy to support your local business." His dad reached for his wallet and Lulu swatted his hand with an adamant refusal.

Preston chuckled, missing the rest of her words. He moved another ornament to a nearby branch as he strained to hear the rest. Apparently, she'd offered to make something custom for his father.

"That's mighty kind of you. A savory donut doesn't sound half-bad. Like a dressed-up bagel, maybe." Dad took a sip of his coffee. Good thing they'd made it decaf—he was really pounding it back.

"What do you think you're doing?"

Preston jumped as his mom came up behind him. "A poor job on the tree, according to you and Lulu." He handed over the dangling candy cane he'd just picked up.

Mom secured it to a branch, casting a knowing glance between him and the window. "Mmm-hmm. You were never good at sneaking around, you know."

He thought of his and Lulu's secret, and the tips of his ears burned. Hopefully for his parents' sake he'd gotten better at it. "I'm glad they get along."

"Me, too. We like her a lot." His mom craned her head to see around the tree, joining his sneaking. "I hope this one sticks."

"As opposed to the last one, who married my brother?"

Mom shook her head. "Now, Preston. That wasn't meant to be."

"I know. Gabrielle and I weren't a good fit." If he didn't miss his ex-girlfriend in the slightest, why did that sense of bitterness spring up every time he thought about how she'd chosen Jackson over him? Preston was genuinely glad he and Gabrielle hadn't ended up together—it would have never worked. They were far too different.

So why the tension between him and Jackson still?

"Everything happens for a reason." Mom turned away from the window and took a deep breath, her eyes glistening as she looked up at him. "Even bad news from doctors."

He wanted to believe that was true. Instead of debating, he pulled her into a hug. "It'll be okay. It was last time." It *had* to be okay. The family wasn't ready for a life without Harold Green. It was far too soon.

"I know." His mother hugged him back, then eased away as she offered a brave smile. "Just keep praying for him."

Preston's throat tightened. That meant he had to get to a place where his prayers actually made it all the way to God.

Which first meant figuring out why they'd stopped.

Lulu came back inside then, breaking up the emotional moment. She smiled at him, and the lump in his throat eased. Funny how she had a way of doing that.

Then her gaze darted past him to the tree and her eyes widened with shock. "Preston! What did you do? I was gone for maybe ten minutes."

He quickly stepped away from the tree, hands up in surrender, as his mom laughed and rejoined his father outside. Then he stood back and watched Lulu work, content to be near her and her running monologue of Tree Trimming 101.

As she rambled on about ornament balance and the proper way to fluff a branch, he breathed a prayer of gratitude for his funny, feisty new friend who cared about his family.

It was a start.

"I've decided what I want to be when I grow up." Hayley released a short breath, sending a few loose tendrils of hair that had come free of her braid fluttering into her face.

"What's that?" Lulu asked, a roll of paper towels in hand as she turned to face the younger girl. She, Claudia, Hayley and Tori had all met up after church to work on the Haven Project jobsite, which had made significant progress since her last visit. The sheetrock had finally been completed, which meant there were a lot of stubborn spackle drips to scrape off before the floors could be laid.

"Wait. You mean, there's life after cheerleading?" Claudia teased, bending down to scrub at a particularly stubborn piece of drywall. The yellow hard hat she wore slipped down over her eyes, and she shoved it back.

"I want to be anything *but* a construction worker." Ignoring Claudia, Hayley resumed sweeping the concrete pad at their feet with a groan. "This is wreaking absolute havoc on my nails."

Judging by what she'd seen so far of Hayley's work ethic, Lulu was pretty sure the construction industry wouldn't want her, either. But she was still proud of the teens for showing up and being involved.

She set the paper towels on a nearby windowsill, nodding a greeting at a fellow volunteer passing through the would-be dining room. "You're doing great, Hayley. Even these little details like cleaning go a long way toward the finished product."

"Yeah, it's all important." Tori tossed an abandoned soda can into an industrial-size trash bag. "Like Mr. Settle keeps telling us." Then she held the bag open for another volunteer to dump their dustpan full of wood shavings.

"Maybe. But he's the foreman. He's supposed to say things like that to inspire us to keep working." Hayley stopped sweeping and leaned into her broom handle. "Look, I'll be honest. I'm doing this mostly for the boost to my college résumés."

"Does doing a good deed count if you don't have the right reason?" Tori asked, squinting.

Lulu bit back a smirk at the dramatically offended expression on Hayley's face. Then she realized Tori was asking *her*, and she winced. The lie she and Preston were currently living in front of his parents felt like the opposite of what the teen had asked, and equally unsettling. She and Preston had the right reason, but were they doing a good thing?

She wanted to think so, but the whole situation turned gray very quickly. "Um… What do you mean by *count*?"

Tori shrugged. "You know, like, to God. Does it count?"

"I think all good deeds count." Claudia took a break from scraping the concrete to grin up at them. "Except maybe Hayley's."

"Ha, ha." Hayley rolled her eyes as she looked down at Claudia. "And will you take off that ridiculous hat? The contractor said we don't have to wear them at this stage of construction. Unless you're on a ladder."

"I know. But it looks cool." Claudia stood and tapped the top of her hard hat. "Fashion statement."

"It's a statement all right, but it's not saying what you think it does," Hayley replied matter-of-factly.

Ignoring their antics, Tori returned her attention to Lulu. "But the pastor at church today talked about motivations. I think the *why* matters."

She slung her arm around Tori's shoulder. "I think it does, too. But he also said that even our best efforts are still usually flawed by pride or some kind of selfishness."

"Like college résumés." Claudia winked. She handed Tori the scraper.

Hayley began sweeping again. "It's okay to want to help people *and* get into a good school."

"But which one do you want the most?" Tori looked worried as she stared at Hayley, scraper in one hand and trash bag gripped in the other.

"And don't lie." Claudia pointed at their flustered friend. "That's a sin, too."

A fresh wave of guilt washed over Lulu. Claudia was teasing, but the fact remained—she and Preston were technically lying.

"Whatever." Hayley waved their teasing off.

"I'm going to go sweep the breakfast nook. Tori, bring the bag."

Lulu tuned out the rest of the girls' bantering as they meandered into the next room, letting her thoughts drift as she scraped more drywall drips from the floor. She didn't like the misleading she and Preston were doing. But she *did* like pretending to date him. There was something so freeing about getting to hang out with a guy friend and feel zero pressure of trying to impress or overthink what he thought of her.

And now that she had managed to stop comparing him with Neal, she was enjoying Preston's company more and more. Decorating the tree yesterday—okay, fixing Preston's mistakes on the tree yesterday—had been fun. After she'd talked with Harold outside and promised to find him a savory donut he could enjoy, she and Preston had cranked up a few Christmas carols and finished off the decaf pot of coffee, sneaking marshmallows into theirs when Harold wasn't looking.

She used the edge of the pole peeler on the drywall, then squatted down to brush the stubborn clumps into a dustpan. She liked Preston's parents—a lot—and felt accepted. Especially by Harold. Susie was nice, too, but she and Harold were connecting a little more easily. She noticed how hard Susie watched him and admired the obvious love and care the woman had for her husband. She also noticed, via Susie's furtive whispers and over-the-top control efforts of everything around them, how they were trying to protect Preston from the reality of what they were really facing. Lulu got the impression the prognosis wasn't quite as hopeful as they were projecting it to be—which made sense with it being recurrent.

Preston was trying to keep his dad safe, yet at the same time, his dad was trying to keep *him* safe. Dysfunctional, maybe, but sweet.

Then again, what did she know? She didn't have a dad who'd bothered to stick around.

"You missed a spot."

Lulu looked up at the familiar voice above her and couldn't help the smile taking command of her cheeks. "Did I?"

Preston extended one hand and she took it, his palm warm in hers. He hauled her to her feet.

She let go reluctantly, attempting but failing to ignore the way her heart rate automatically increased in his presence. "You're welcome to take over."

"Put me to work." He made a show of dusting off his sleeves. "That's what we came for."

She noticed Aiden for the first time, standing slightly behind Preston. "Oh, hey! It's good to see you."

The boy nodded, avoiding eye contact as he shuffled his feet. "Just point me to a broom."

"Claudia and the others are in the breakfast area around the corner." Lulu pointed. "They'll get you set up."

He nodded, head down as he followed her direction.

"And, Aiden?"

He turned, his thin shoulders slightly hunched inside his T-shirt.

"Don't let Hayley boss you around *too* much."

A ghost of a grin flickered across his face, and he nodded. "Yes, ma'am."

Preston took the pole peeler from Lulu. "I was on my way here and saw him out wandering around Main Street. He looked bored, so I thought it might be good for him to come lend a hand since you said the project was still behind."

Lulu looked in the direction Aiden had disappeared. "Good call bringing him along. I'm still worried about him. He's not the same as he was this past summer. Something's changed."

"He's a teenage boy." Preston shrugged. "Which means he probably doesn't want to talk about it. Maybe a relationship issue. He could have gotten dumped recently."

"I've never seen him date anyone—he just hangs out with Claudia, Hayley and Tori." Lulu sighed. "I don't know. I just have a bad feeling."

"I'll keep an eye on him." Preston reached out and lightly touched her shoulder. "Speaking of dating…" He lowered his voice. "Do you think it'll raise suspicion to the teens that I'm here at the jobsite with you again?"

She hadn't thought of that. The last thing they needed for their ruse was to bring more people into the mix. Lulu paused, then slowly shook her head. "They know I try to get practically everyone I meet to volunteer here. I doubt they'll think anything of it." She hesitated. "I'm glad you came, though. Where are your parents?"

"Dad's napping, and Mom took the opportunity to run out and look at some gift shops on Main Street. That's when I saw Aiden. She insisted I leave her there for a few hours to browse, so I could go find you."

She immediately missed the feel of his hand on her shoulder, and her face flushed remembering their brief conversation about PDA just a few nights ago. She quickly tried to redirect her thoughts. *It isn't real.* "I'm sorry you all had to miss church this morning."

"Yeah, Dad didn't feel great. He pretended like it was no big deal, but I wonder." Preston lifted one shoulder in a shrug. "You'll have to fill me in on the sermon later."

"I will." Her stomach fluttered at his proximity, and she realized she was in very real danger of getting distracted by him if she didn't get back to work. She gave him a gentle shove toward the dustpan. "Off you go. The mess is that way."

He laughed. "Do I need to punch a timecard to get credit for today?"

"It counts, don't worry." She nudged him again.

"One more thing." He turned so quickly, he nearly bumped into her.

She took a step back and tripped over her own foot, but his hand lightly gripped her arm and kept her steady. And close. Close enough to detect the scent of his cologne. For a moment, she knew he had spoken, but for the life of her she couldn't remember what he'd said. Even the sounds of the construction crew and their electric drills running in the partially completed rooms around them faded to a dull drone. It was her, and him, and the softness of his shirt beneath her hand that had somehow come to land on his chest.

Oh, this wasn't good at all.

She jerked her arm away. "What's that?" She lifted her chin but kept her expression neutral, forcing all evidence of her inner tumult away.

He was staring back down at her, as if he'd also forgotten what he was about to say. "I was just going to tell you my mom has a surprise double date planned for us this week." He sounded a little dazed, but that was probably just the lingering effects of her heartbeat roaring in her ears. "I'll keep you posted on the details, but I have a feeling she won't be giving me many. She likes planning things like that."

"Sounds fun." And a little like torture, if this overwhelming wave of attraction didn't fizzle by then. She took a tight breath, releasing the flood of feelings. "Hopefully your dad will enjoy it."

"I'm sure he will." Preston laughed. "He likes whatever Mom tells him to, anyway."

Her return smile felt more genuine now, her body relaxing. "They're cute."

"Thirty-three years married and going strong. Mom started planning their fiftieth anniversary party last year." His smile wavered a little after his last words, and she could hear the rest of the fear he didn't speak.

Hopefully his dad would be around to attend.

She fought the urge to wrap him in a hug, afraid of what the contact would do to her rollercoaster emotions. Instead, she patted his arm, then turned him gently toward the breakfast nook. "One thing at a time."

She needed to take her own advice.

Chapter Ten

If he was expected to decorate a gingerbread house in an hour, he was going to need more coffee. Preston checked the pot his mom had made earlier that afternoon, then realized it would most likely be decaf. That wasn't going to cut it—not to gear up for yet another outing with Lulu and his parents. His mom had accidentally let a detail slip for their surprise date that night, and apparently, it involved gingerbread. Lots and lots of gingerbread.

He quickly dumped the bottom dredges of the carafe and prepared a fresh pot, his conscience ticking the whole time. Like a time bomb? Hopefully not. So far, their ruse was going perfectly. His parents believed he and Lulu were in a serious relationship, and his dad had never seemed more relaxed. Even while piddling around Tulip Mound, following his mom in and out of all the stores and insisting on carrying her bags, Dad seemed to be thriving. Of course, he needed to sit down a lot more often than he used to, but for the most part, he seemed to be doing all right. Maybe this holiday break had been good for him, after all.

And at the end of the day, Preston would much rather his conscience suffer than his dad's health.

He wandered into the living room while waiting for the coffee to brew, half anticipating and half dreading the upcoming holiday extravaganza his mom had planned. It was like she'd watched a dozen of those made-for-TV Christmas movies before arriving in Tulip Mound and was personally dedicated to recreating each one.

He couldn't complain about the extra time with Lulu, though. He enjoyed being around her more and more.

Preston rounded the corner and found his father sitting in the recliner, balancing a plate of donuts on his lap. "Where'd you get those?"

"Get what?" He pretended to stash the plate beside the chair.

"Those were Oopsy Daisy donuts, weren't they?"

"They are. Special-menu items." His dad pulled the plate back onto his lap. "I can't eat another bite, though. I've already had two." He patted his stomach. "Don't tell your mother."

Preston eyed the two pastries remaining on the plate and couldn't readily identify any of Lulu's usual recipes. "Are those dark chocolate?" She must have dyed something in the mix for the holidays, because scatters of green, almost like confetti pieces, broke the consistency of the dough. Interesting choice.

"Something like that." Dad extended the plate. "Here. Help yourself."

He never used to like donuts—before Lulu, that is. But he couldn't resist the opportunity to try a special-menu item and let her know how he liked it. He plucked one and took a bite.

Then his eyes widened. Definitely not dark chocolate.

A spicy, entirely unpleasant sensation filled his mouth, then his throat. He couldn't swallow, but there was nowhere to spit. And the salt... What was crunchy? He fought every impulse in his body and gulped the lingering bite down. "*Dad.* What in the world?"

His father guffawed, laughing so hard his face turned red. "Gotcha."

His mouth was burning. He needed water. Or rather, a sponge to scrub his tongue. Preston quickly rushed back to the kitchen and chugged a half glass of milk, then poured his waiting coffee before returning to the living room and his still-amused father. "Very funny."

"Salty, huh?"

"And spicy." He sipped his coffee, then made a face at the aftertaste. "You ate two? Or was that part of the prank?"

"They taste good to me." His father shrugged, leaning forward in the recliner to sit upright. "Jalapeño potato chip."

That explained the salty-spicy combo. "Lulu made those for you?"

"She asked me the other night what type of flavors I appreciated. She knew chemo patients sometimes have some pretty roughed-up taste buds, and she wanted to do something nice for me." Dad shook his head. "You've got a keeper in that one, son."

She'd done all that...just for his dad? It certainly wasn't as if she could have sold the others from the batch. It was a selfless investment on her part. Preston stared into his coffee, surprised yet at the same time, not surprised at all. Lulu continued to prove herself more and more as a person of noble character. Radiating genuine concern and goodness.

And he just continued to lie. How long could he keep this up? His stomach flipped. "Dad..."

"Yeah?" His father raised one bushy eyebrow.

The rest of his confession died on his tongue, and he swallowed, still tasting the remains of the lethal donut. He could tell the truth right now and avoid this whole gingerbread extravaganza. He could go to the Christmas service at church with a clean conscience. Maybe then God would hear his prayers again.

But what if he told the truth and it backfired? What if he confessed and his dad got upset and his health plummeted? His father seemed to really like Lulu. At this point, he'd feel tricked. Maybe even betrayed. And at what cost? His healthy vitals for Preston's ease of mind?

His dad had always been there for him. Surely, Preston could ride this out a little longer for him in return.

He took a deep breath. "You have donut crumbs on your shirt."

His father glanced down and brushed away the evidence of his dessert. Then he met Preston's gaze and held it. "Is that all?"

He stared back, half-paralyzed, refusing to lie directly to his dad's face but unable to tell the truth. "I—"

"Ready to go?" His mom bustled into the room with a smile, wearing her favorite Jingle All the Way sweatshirt with the linked candy canes she'd owned for at least a decade. "Lulu should be here any minute." The doorbell rang, and she laughed. "Well, that was perfect timing."

Preston released a sigh of relief as he stood to get the door.

Perfect timing, indeed.

She was *not* falling for Preston. She was helping a friend.

Lulu repeated the mantra in her mind as she sat in the back seat of his parents' sedan, feeling a little like a middle schooler about to get dropped off on a group date. Except this wasn't a date—to anyone except Harold and Susie, anyway. Definitely not to Preston.

And it shouldn't be to her.

She stared out the window at the passing scenery as they headed through the outskirts of Tulip Mound to their secret destination. Susie had refused to give them a hint, even though Preston seemed to think it had something to do with gingerbread.

"You okay? You're quiet." Preston's voice, just a notch above a whisper, was shielded by the Christmas music Susie had blaring from the radio.

"Just thinking. And tired—it was a busy day at the shop." All truths. She refused to lie any more than what it felt like they were already doing.

"I really appreciate you doing this." He kept

his tone a low hum, despite the current blast of "All I Want for Christmas."

"I'm happy to help." She avoided touching Preston's hand that rested on the middle seat between them, despite feeling its proximity down to her marrow. Did he feel the attraction, too? Sometimes she wondered…like this past Sunday at the Haven Project site. They seemed to have a connection, but she wasn't good at reading those things. He was probably just acting.

But what if he *wasn't*? She tried to return her focus to the conversation. "I'm sure whatever your mom has planned will be fun."

He let out a slow breath. "Let's hope so."

"I'm enjoying being around them." She hesitated, making sure his parents were engaged in conversation before daring to speak her next words. "It almost feels unnecessary."

"What?"

"This whole fake-date thing. It's obvious your parents care about you."

"Of course they do." He ran a hand over his hair. "But you saw how different things were when Jackson was around."

He adjusted the seat belt strap across his chest, lowering his voice as the station changed to "Santa Baby." "Regardless of all that, my dad really likes you. He talks about you every time you leave."

The thought warmed her all the way through. Harold was a great dad. She didn't know a lot about how fathers were supposed to be but she had a feeling he was top-notch. "He says good things, I hope."

"Almost annoyingly so." Preston nudged her. She grinned. "I really like him, too."

"I can tell." Preston held her gaze for a moment, studying her, until she had to look away. "And I'm grateful."

Not falling. Helping a friend.

Susie turned down the radio then and asked Preston a question about work, saving Lulu from further evaluation. She leaned her head back against the seat rest as the snow-dusted tree branches whipped past the vehicle.

Awkward as it was riding in the back, there was also something strangely comforting about it. She didn't have many memories—make that zero pleasant ones—of feeling safe with two parents in the front seat. Her dad had left when she was so young, along with a sense of security. Her mom had let her ride in the front a little sooner than was wise, just to have the company. Which made Lulu feel grown-up...*and* also made her feel the pressure that came with needing to be.

At least that was one plus that had come from Operation Mistletoe—getting to know Harold a little better.

Accidentally finding herself more and more attracted to Preston was, however, *not* a plus.

The car slowed, then turned into a long driveway. "We're here!" Susie announced.

"Here?" Preston leaned forward to look out the window.

Lulu frowned, following his gaze. Jitter Mugs? Susie couldn't have possibly driven them all this way just for coffee. Tori's uncle Blake owned the sprawling, hybrid property that was part coffee shop, part event venue and part dog shelter. Sure, he had a delicious list of holiday brews, but how did Susie even know this place existed?

"What is this?" Preston asked.

Then the parking lot full of cars, some spilling over into the frost-speckled yard, registered with Lulu. As did the throng of people milling about the front doors and the lit back deck, which was draped in twinkle lights and lined with space heaters. It looked like half the town had shown up for—

"Tulip Mound's annual gingerbread decorating contest!" Susie declared as she pulled into one of the last spaces available and cut the engine. "Surprise!"

"The surprise is going to be when they see my lack of artistic ability," Harold mumbled with a grin as he unbuckled his seat belt. "Do we at least get to eat the candy?"

Preston shot a worried look at Lulu, which she didn't quite get. Was he concerned about his dad being in a crowd, getting overly tired? His parents climbed out of the car, and before Lulu could follow suit, Preston tugged at her elbow.

She twisted in the seat to face him and raised her eyebrows.

"Everyone is here," he whispered. His dark hair, always perfectly styled, looked as wilted as his expression.

Her stomach clenched. Was he afraid to be seen with her?

"Looks that way." Lulu tried to shrug like she didn't care, but the warmth radiating up her arm at his touch seemed to prevent her shoulder from obeying her brain.

He didn't let go. *"Everyone,"* he repeated.

Then the fog cleared. Everyone was there… including Tori and Claudia and the other teenagers…who knew Preston. Who knew her.

And who did *not* know they were pretend dating.

Chapter Eleven

Maybe they wouldn't see them.

Lulu kept her head ducked as she icing-glued gumdrops to her fragile gingerbread roof. Preston wasn't kidding when he said everyone had turned out for the big contest. She'd already spotted Blake and Charlie across the crowded room, which meant Tori had to be nearby. And if she was there, it seemed inevitable her friends would be. Even Rachel, who managed Paradise Paws, was sitting with Principal Crowder at a nearby table.

Everyone seemed to be having a good time, but Lulu really just hoped the teens didn't catch sight of her and Preston. How in the world would they be able to keep up the charade in front of his mom and dad, without looking too chummy in front of the girls? They'd seen her and Preston together at the jobsite, but attending a holiday event with his parents had a different connotation.

"You missed a spot."

Her icing tube jerked, knocking into her precarious cookie walls. The house teetered, but didn't fall, and she breathed a sigh of relief as she turned to swat at Preston's arm. "Quit doing that!"

"I just hope the crew at the Haven Project doesn't find out about this." He made a tsking sound as he leaned back in his own chair and continued piping. "That's pretty shoddy construction work you have there."

She stifled a laugh. "I could do a much better job with this thing if I had a hammer and nails instead of dried sugar and butter."

"But then you couldn't eat your mistakes." Preston popped a bite of broken gingerbread into his mouth, and she couldn't help but smile.

"If you re-pipe the icing, then hold the walls together for a minute, they dry faster." Across the table, Susie demonstrated her tip to Lulu.

She followed suit. "That does work. Thank you."

Susie waved off the gratitude with a flip of her hand. "I've made a dozen of these things over the years, so I know all the hacks. Of course, you know baking better than I do, but I imagine there's no glue involved with your donuts."

"Glue. Hmm. Now that might be a preferable flavor compared to that chocolate jalapeño potato chip invention." Preston shot Lulu a wink, and her stomach incinerated. Now she officially wasn't sure which was the biggest disaster—her gingerbread house attempt, or her roller-coaster feelings at Preston's proximity.

"Well, I'm happy to hear your father shared." She kept her tone light and her gaze on the cookie roof beneath her hands, though she ached to meet Preston's eyes and try to interpret the light dancing in them. But that'd be dangerous. Right now, she'd use any excuse she could to convince herself that he wasn't acting anymore. That he felt the same herd of flying reindeer in his stomach that she felt every time his arm brushed against hers, every time his low voice muttered something meant only for her to hear.

And she couldn't risk that.

"I might have had an ulterior motive with sharing." Harold laughed. "The look on Preston's face was well worth the sacrifice."

"Very funny." Preston looped his arm around the back of Lulu's chair and leaned in close. "Maybe warn a guy the next time you invent a new donut, hmm?"

She couldn't help it this time—she turned her head to look at him. He was smiling, leaning in close, his eyes shining with…admiration. Humor.

And flirtatiousness.

Her heart jumped into her throat then nose-dived into the depths. He was definitely flirting. She might not have a lot of experience in that area, but the way he looked at her…it was obvious.

The looming question remained—were his feelings becoming genuine, or was it still just a show for his parents?

But if that were the case, shouldn't he be pulling back in case they ran into anyone else they knew here?

She had no way to know. If only she could have some kind of sign…

A red-and-green paper chain suddenly descended around Lulu's shoulders. She jerked away from Preston and grabbed for the ends as someone draped them loosely around her neck like a scarf and giggled.

"What—" She turned in her chair to find Tori standing behind her, laughing.

Claudia flanked her to the left, chewing her way through a handful of marshmallows. "Hey, Teach." She nodded at Preston, and her gaze darted between him and Lulu as he slowly removed his arm from the back of her chair. Claudia raised her eyebrows.

Oh, no. Lulu sucked in a small breath. This was exactly what she'd been afraid of.

Beside her, she felt Preston stiffen. "Hey,

gang." His voice sounded natural, at least, but his eyes flitted to his parents, who hadn't seemed to notice the girls yet.

Thankfully, Tori didn't seem to notice them, either. She unwound the chain from Lulu while Hayley, standing to Tori's right, adjusted her pom beanie and sniffed. "There's a craft table over there for the little kids," Hayley explained. "She couldn't resist."

"You can hang it in Oopsy Daisy if you want." Tori took the empty seat next to Lulu, and Claudia draped over the back of her chair. Her long-sleeved T-shirt today read Jingle Bell Rock, featuring a giant guitar decorated in holly berries and bold music notes.

"So what's new?" Claudia knowingly looked back and forth between Lulu and Preston again as if she could already guess.

Susie glanced up. "Preston, are these some of your students?"

"Yes, ma'am. He's our history teacher." Tori popped a red M&M in her mouth.

"And you're the mom?" Claudia asked.

Susie laughed. "I'm the mom. And this is the dad." She elbowed Harold, who was focused on lining up his peppermint roof decorations.

"Nice to meet you ladies." He held out a bowl of lemon drops. "Anyone?"

Hayley crossed her arms over her jacket. "No

thanks. And I think these two have already had enough."

"That's the other mom." Claudia rolled her eyes.

She took a lemon candy and tossed it at Hayley. It bounced off her jacket and landed on the ground. Hayley cocked an eyebrow at her. "Really?"

"Anyways." Claudia turned her back to Hayley. "As I was saying… What's new?" She tilted her head toward Preston, her eyes calculating.

"Are we just going to ignore the fact that she threw candy at me?" Hayley asked.

"Now, ladies, remember what we've been learning about the brutalities of war." Preston gestured between Claudia and Hayley. "That's not how we do things, is it?"

Lulu couldn't tell if he was being serious with the life-lesson attempt, or just trying to distract Claudia from continuing down her current line of questioning. Regardless, she had to act fast. She stood. "Preston—I mean, Mr. Green—is right."

Hayley and Claudia turned to her in surprise.

"I mean, he's been teasing me about my gingerbread house all evening, and I haven't done a thing about it in retaliation," she continued.

"See? Peacekeeping." Preston nodded with a satisfied smile.

"Until now." Lulu grabbed a fistful of miniature M&M's and flung them at Preston. The tiny colored orbs hit him directly in the chest, some sliding down the neck of his sweater before bouncing off his lap and then the ground.

He gasped. Claudia and Hayley stared. Tori clapped her hand over her mouth. Harold and Susie blinked rapidly.

No one moved, save for the M&M's continuing to fall one by one to the floor.

The silence stretched, and Lulu's heart dropped toward her ankle boots. What kind of example was she setting—and in front of Preston's parents, no less?

"Well." Preston stood, the rest of the candies plinking to the floor. He was using what Lulu already recognized as his teacher voice. Judging by Tori's wide eyes and Claudia's slow retreat, she figured they recognized it, too. "I guess there's only one thing to say."

Lulu shifted her weight, candy crunching under her boots. "I'm really sorr—"

"Food fight!" Preston scooped a handful of the lemon drops from the table and showered them upon Lulu. She ducked, then grabbed for fresh ammo.

Claudia armed herself with more marshmallows, while Hayley squealed. Tori took the opportunity to nab M&M's, and alternated peppering them at Lulu and Hayley, who held her hands defensively over her carefully curled hair and yelled stats about the casualties of World War II.

Harold cracked up, his whole body shaking with laughter as he scooted his chair away from the fray. Susie handed Lulu a bowl with a few remaining Hershey Kisses inside and winked.

"I see you aiding and abetting the enemy there, Mom." Preston reached for the cup of Skittles, but Lulu snatched them out of his reach just in time. Soon, an unofficial alliance formed as everyone turned their edible weapons on Preston. Harold joined in, chucking some of the candy wrappers his son's way. Hayley scooted under the table.

Preston dived toward the ground. "Truce!"

Breathless, Lulu held up her empty hands. "I think it's time for a cease-fire, guys."

Preston cautiously lifted his head from behind the folding chair. "Good thing midterms are already graded." He stood and brushed off his pants.

"I'm sticky." Tori held up her color-streaked hands.

Claudia steered her toward the restrooms in the back. "Let's go wash up."

"I'm coming with you." Hayley emerged from the table.

"I'll go get more candy." Susie took some of their empty bowls and made her way toward the front of the community room.

Preston stood beside Lulu, a lemon drop balanced on one shoulder. She brushed it off. "You better go clean up, too, *Teach*."

"That was fun." He looked at his dad, then at the girls walking away, before returning his gaze to Lulu. "Be right back." Then he dropped a kiss on the top of her head and was gone.

Trying to hide her beaming smile, she collapsed into a chair across from Harold, breathless and unsure if it was from the food fight or from that *thing* Preston had just done. So casually. So naturally. She couldn't help but watch him stroll through the maze of tables toward the restrooms, all broad shoulders and tousled hair.

She'd just been given her sign.

"You're good for my boy." Harold chuckled as he scooped the candy casualties scattered over the table into another bowl. "He never had fun like that with Gabrielle. She kept him too stuffy."

"Gabrielle?" Lulu abruptly turned to face Harold. He must mean Preston hung out with Gabrielle and Jackson when they first started dating. But that picture didn't quite add up to Preston and Jackson's current relationship. They didn't seem like the cozy double-dating type. She frowned.

The older man nodded, seemingly oblivious to her confusion as he wiped his icing-coated fingers on a paper towel. "Yeah, but Jackson doesn't let Gabrielle get to him like Preston did. Jackson is his own person, and she adapts to it. Their dynamic is much healthier."

Now she was really confused. The comparison he made almost sounded as if Gabrielle and Preston—

"We all knew that relationship was doomed from the beginning." Harold gestured his finger between Lulu and the direction Preston had walked. "Not like this one. Don't worry."

Her cheeks heated, and suddenly the neck of her sweater felt like it might choke her. Harold was still talking, something about "the way he looks at you," but the words bounced off like tiny pinballs as his previous statement landed a direct hit.

Gabrielle and Preston used to date.

Her heart twisted. Why hadn't he told her? Of course, that relationship was obviously ancient history, considering how Gabrielle and Jackson just got married, but Preston's motivation in not wanting to be single at Christmas made a lot more sense now.

And so did the grim reality that she was way off base.

Despite their connection and all the fun outings, Preston didn't truly like her. Or *like*-like her, as the teenagers would say. She and Preston were friends, and anything beyond that was mere pretending for his parents' sake. Including that quick kiss he'd just planted on her.

She'd been given a sign, all right.

The burn of tears pressed behind her eyes, and she blinked it away. She didn't need to stand next to elegant, sophisticated, well-spoken Gabrielle for the drastic differences between them to be vivid. No wonder she knew about his mushroom allergy. Any good girlfriend would—and Gabrielle had actually been his girlfriend.

If Preston had been hung up on Gabrielle enough at one point to need a fake date in her presence for Christmas dinner, it was clear Lulu was not—and would never be—his type.

She took a deep breath and popped a Jolly Rancher in her mouth. It was a good thing she realized all this now, before she humiliated herself further. Before she'd gotten herself too emotionally involved.

Or at least, that's what she would keep telling herself until she meant it.

Chapter Twelve

"Did you and Lulu have a fight?" Mom's soft voice wasn't quite low enough for Preston's preference, despite the sounds of construction around them as they strolled through the space that would eventually be the kitchen—if the cabinets ever got installed. She'd wanted to see the progress on the Haven Project, after hearing Lulu talk about it so much over the past week, so he had reluctantly agreed to bring her by the construction site when he and Lulu went next.

However, he hadn't realized that the next time they went, Lulu would be barely speaking to him.

"Why do you ask?" Preston avoided answering directly, because honestly, he didn't know. Lulu had seemed off ever since the evening of the gingerbread contest a few days prior. And it wasn't because Noah from the Hummingbird

Inn had won the grand prize for the night. She'd been polite but distant on the entire drive home, which he'd chalked up to her being tired and maybe on a bit of a sugar crash.

But now, after two days of her making excuses not to come over and eat Mexican food with his family last night or go holiday shopping with them the day before that, he had a sinking feeling he knew what had gone wrong.

That kiss.

"Just haven't seen her in a few days, that's all." Mom stopped next to the taped X on the concrete that indicated where the island would be installed. "You seemed to have fun together the other night."

"Of course." Preston uneasily ran his hand through his hair, hoping that Lulu, who was helping measure window trim in the next room, couldn't hear their conversation. "We always do."

Not a lie. He made a point not to when talking about the details of his and Lulu's relationship. They weren't dating—but he *did* always have a good time when she was around.

Except maybe today. She'd said very few words when they met up at the jobsite, and had gone straight to work, sticking close to the contractor, Micah Settle.

Preston had obviously pushed her too far. It had seemed like the most natural thing in the world when he'd dropped that kiss on her head. His spirits had felt as high as Santa's sleigh after the big food fight, and he'd gotten swept up in the fun and the connection with her. But they hadn't discussed the topic of PDA boundaries since that first night they'd started this whole charade at his house, and he'd clearly taken it too far. He needed to apologize for overstepping, but she hadn't exactly made it easy to do so—and it seemed like a copout to just send a text.

The part she could never know was that he hadn't done it for show but because he wanted to. Or that he really wanted to do it again. Properly. Which was problematic, because in about six months, he wouldn't even be living in Tulip Mound anymore.

His mother cleared her throat, bringing him away from the memory and back to the in-progress kitchen. "I'm glad you two seem to be getting serious."

More like he was seriously getting in over his head. He offered a noncommittal sound, refusing to confirm or deny.

"Your father and I really like her."

The mention of his father sent a sudden ripple of unease through Preston's stomach. Instead of joining them at the jobsite, Dad had chosen to stay at Preston's house in the recliner he'd all but claimed this trip, eager to watch TV and nap—which meant he was starting to overdo it.

He took a deep breath. "Mom, I was thinking…about Dad."

"Yes?" She didn't look at him as she ran one hand over the barn door that transitioned the kitchen to the dining room. Her features were already schooled into that no-nonsense expression of denial she always wore when dealing with something she didn't like. "This grain sure is pretty." She patted the wood.

He ignored the attempt at redirection. "I think Dad might be doing too much. Maybe we should pull back a little on all these holiday outings."

She waved one hand in the air. "He's fine. He just likes that chair of yours. I'm thinking of ordering him one like it for Christmas. Where did you get it?" She pulled out her phone and opened a note app to document his answer.

"It came furnished with the cottage." Something was definitely up—that was two attempts at changing the subject. "I'm serious. I think he needs some rest before Christmas."

Her features went brittle as she slid her phone into her pocket. "He's getting plenty of rest."

"Mom—"

She slapped one hand against the door. "I'm handling it!" Then her eyes widened, and she sucked in a breath. "I'm sorry."

"No, it's okay." He knew when to back off. "It's my fault. I pushed."

"You're concerned." Compassion filled her eyes, and she touched his arm. "But we've walked through this before, all right? I know what he needs."

He wanted to believe that, but he also knew how badly his mother needed to believe she had control where she simply didn't.

But instead of saying so, he quietly pulled her into a hug. She hugged him back, then sniffed and edged away, dabbing under her eye with one finger. "Speaking of your father, I think I better go on home. Well, to *your* home."

"I'm really glad you guys are here." He could say that and mean it now, with his full heart. Operation Mistletoe or not, he was grateful they were together this holiday. His throat tightened and he refused to follow that train of thought to its next natural stop.

Once again, the urge to tell the truth welled up in his throat. But his mom's emotional stability didn't seem ready for such a blow—and neither did his dad's health. What had made so much sense just a week ago now just felt like a giant mistake.

Troubled, he walked his mom to the front entrance just as Aiden, Claudia and Hayley strolled up the hill of the dirt "yard."

"Hey, Teach." Claudia slapped him a high five as she breezed into the house, Hayley on her heels, prattling on about hard hats.

"Hey, girls." Preston waved goodbye to his mom, then stepped back to allow Aiden, who was trailing after the young women, into the house. The teen nodded at Preston and said a subdued greeting before scurrying after his friends.

Preston frowned, watching him follow them into the kitchen. The guy sure must like navy T-shirts. Preston wasn't typically one to notice who wore what—except lately, when he kept noticing Lulu's holiday gear and how cute she looked in it—but he hadn't seen Aiden in anything but those blue shirts for a while now. In fact, quite possibly the *same* shirt, because one of the sleeve seams was unraveling, and it hung noticeably longer on that arm.

Aiden didn't even wear a jacket most days, which wasn't unusual for high school boys— Preston remembered he tried to wear shorts in December when he was that age—but Aiden didn't seem to be the stubborn, prove-a-point kind of kid. In fact, the way he walked hunched into himself, he looked…cold.

Once the young man rounded the house into the kitchen, out of sight, Preston quickly unlocked his car with his key fob. Then he opened the passenger door and scanned the back seat. There it was. He'd gotten a stain on his favorite jacket and had worn an older one the other day when shopping with his parents. He didn't need it…and it looked like Aiden did.

He draped the dark fabric over his arm and headed back inside, trying to figure out the best way to go about his mission without embarrassing the guy. He found the teenagers with Lulu in the living room, gathered around the sawhorse bearing the trim she and Micah had cut.

Preston stifled a grin. Lulu wore safety goggles and a knitted cap, and with her yellow scarf still draped around her neck, looked like a cartoon character.

"Perfect cut." Micah ran his hand over the trim. "Not bad for a first-timer."

"Thanks." Lulu grinned, then her gaze met Preston's and she quickly whipped off the goggles, as if only then realizing he was there. "Is there another piece?"

"There are a lot of pieces." Micah shook his head, gesturing to the windows lining the back wall and looking slightly overwhelmed. "I have two crew members sick today, so we can use the extra help. I'll get you set up with the next few, and you can do exactly what you just did. No minors using the miter saw, though, okay?"

"Nice." Claudia nudged Lulu as Micah hurried away. "You're, like, actually doing important stuff."

"Hey, cleaning is important, too." Then Hayley's know-it-all air faded, and she beamed. "But Claudia's right. This is total girl boss of you."

Preston watched the way Lulu laughingly brushed off the praise, thinking the kids weren't the only ones impressed with her. But while the girls fawned over Lulu's new skill, he took the opportunity to call Aiden to the side. Leading him just around the corner to the kitchen, he considered lying about the coat to help Aiden's pride. Telling the kid something along the lines of he found it, and no one had claimed it, so Aiden might as well take it. But Preston was tired of mistruths and half-truths.

Aiden deserved a man-to-man conversation.

"Did I do something wrong?" The teen's brow furrowed and he anxiously shifted his weight.

"Of course not." Preston crossed his arms over his chest, the jacket pressed tight against his sweater. "Unless there's something you want to tell me?" He chuckled.

"No." Aiden's cheeks flushed. "It's just, you know—you're the teacher."

"We're not in class. And you're one of my best students, Aiden." Preston dipped his head and lowered his voice. "I just wanted to make sure everything was okay."

"Okay?" the high schooler parroted, avoiding eye contact.

"Yeah, is everything going all right? With friends. Girls. At home. Whatever."

A shadow flickered across the teen's expression, but it quickly vanished. "All good. Just hanging out during my break."

Preston repressed a sigh. The kid wasn't cracking, and he had already pushed two people he cared about too far the past few days. He wasn't going to push a third. "If that changes, I'm here if you need to talk. I know more than just World War II stats."

"Though probably not as many as Hayley." Aiden finally smiled.

Preston laughed. "Fair." He extended the jacket, done with pretenses. "Why don't you take this off my hands for me?"

Aiden hesitated.

Preston held it out farther. "It would really help me out if you took this."

The kid slowly reached for the coat. "How much?"

"It's not my color, man. You're the one doing me a favor." Preston kept his tone light.

Aiden took it, a knowing look in his eyes. "Thank you." He immediately slipped it on, and a sigh escaped as he wrapped up into its warmth.

Preston leaned against the doorframe. "Thank

you. And hey, I mean it when I said you can talk. Anytime, okay?"

Aiden opened his mouth, then closed it.

Was he cracking? Preston didn't want to miss the opportunity. "I'm all about respecting someone's privacy, but just so you know—secrets can be dangerous."

Aiden warily met his gaze. "How so?"

"Well, depending on what it is, it might hurt the one keeping it. Might put them in a detriment of some kind." Preston shrugged. "Or, at the least, it can get really heavy. Burdens aren't meant to be carried alone."

He shuffled his feet. "Actually—"

A singsong voice suddenly cut in from the other room. *"Lulu and Teacher, sitting in a tree..."*

Oh, no.

Heat crept up Lulu's cheeks as Claudia and Hayley teased her, which she knew only egged them on further. She unplugged the miter saw—this was definitely not the time to be using power tools—and waved her hand at the girls, who were supposed to be gathering trash and sweeping but hadn't picked up a single soda can yet. "Hang on a second."

They finally stopped their chant, but not their giant, knowing grins.

"Why exactly do you think we're dating?" Lulu didn't want to lie, but she couldn't tell the truth, either. Especially now, when her hopes that they *could* actually be dating were freshly dashed. It was all getting so complicated.

Mostly within her heart.

"Well, you're not exactly subtle." Hayley crossed her arms over her thin frame, her red lips carving into a knowing smile. "You're always together now. Here, around town, at the gingerbread contest."

Claudia smirked, an empty industrial-size trash bag resting at her feet. "Not to mention he *kissed* you the other night, right in front of everyone."

There was that. Not that Lulu needed the reminder. She could still feel the impression on her head from his lips. The heat in her cheeks increased tenfold, and she fought the urge to fan her face. They'd never let her live it down.

"Don't worry, we think it's cute." Claudia gestured between herself and Hayley. "Tori, most of all. Says you remind her of her Uncle Blake and Charlie when they were dating a year ago."

Lulu cleared her throat. "Where is Tori, anyway?"

"She had to help her uncle at Jitter Mugs today." Hayley pointed at her with a candy-cane-striped nail. "But don't think you can change the subject."

"Change what subject?" Preston and Aiden came back into the partially completed living room, and Lulu's heart wrung like a wet rag. She'd been avoiding seeing him since her realization the other night, to give herself time to recover and regroup.

Apparently, two days wasn't long enough.

"Just in time." Claudia waggled her eyebrows and rubbed her hands together like an old-fashioned villain in a movie.

"The secret's out." Hayley flipped her ponytail off her shoulder. "We were just telling Lulu that we think you guys make a great couple."

"We...do?" Preston's panicked gaze found Lulu's, as if he wasn't sure which script to follow.

"Definitely. I don't know why you two tried to keep it a secret in the first place." Claudia shrugged.

"Yeah, we think it's great. And you're so cute, double-dating with your parents!" Hayley bounced on the heels of her Converse.

"Wait, you two are together?" Aiden gestured between Lulu and Preston. "I missed something."

"Boys." Hayley shook her head with a tsk. "Keep up, Aiden. It's super obvious."

Lulu took a deep breath, searching Preston's eyes for any kind of indication of how they should proceed. Should they straighten the teens out and end this rumor right here, or play along? The teens had already met Harold and Susie the other night, and the odds of the kids running into Preston's parents in town again during their visit were high, especially during the Christmas Eve service when the whole town would gather for the Home for the Holidays giveaway.

Which looked like it might not be done in time.

Lulu glanced around at all the unfinished projects and made an executive decision. There was no more time to waste on this. It would be a lot easier, and faster, to play along and get everyone back to work. The Haven Project had to take priority over everything else. Plus, if they tried to explain the whole charade now, the kids would have a ton of questions, and then they'd be trusting them with a secret that Lulu couldn't ask them to keep.

"I guess we might as well confess." Lulu moved to stand beside Preston, her heart pounding in her chest. She squared her shoulders and looked up at him, silently beseeching him to play along. "We *were* keeping it a secret, just because it was all so new."

"Ha! Told you so!" Claudia grinned.

Hayley smirked. "You mean, *I* told *you*."

Preston nodded slowly. "Right. So, I guess the, uh, present is out of Santa's bag now."

"Wait. I thought that was a cat." Claudia frowned.

"So your relationship was a *secret*, huh?" Aiden's voice rose uncharacteristically over the others', and his eyes lasered in on Preston. His jaw tightened. "I see." Then he abruptly turned and walked out of the room, hunching into a jacket that was a little too big.

"What was *that* all about?" Claudia asked as the front door of the house slammed shut.

Lulu wanted to know the same. She'd never heard Aiden get upset before, and judging by his teacher's slumped shoulders, it was a big deal to him, too.

Preston sighed. "That was what you'd call really bad timing."

"What happened?" Lulu asked.

He just shook his head and mouthed the word *later*.

A quick glance confirmed Hayley and Claudia were back to arguing over who knows what, so Lulu shifted her back to the girls so only Preston could see her face. "Was that your jacket?" She kept her voice down.

Preston nodded, still looking slightly miserable at whatever had just transpired between him and Aiden. "He needed it more. We almost had a breakthrough, but... Well, I think I just messed that up."

A wave of compassion rose in her heart. Preston had not only kept up his part of the deal by volunteering at the Haven Project for multiple hours, but he'd also taken to heart her request to check up on the Aiden, and he obviously cared about him.

And she'd treated Preston poorly the last few days, all because of an attraction she felt that wasn't even his fault. It wasn't like he was trying to be charming on purpose. He was simply keeping up their arrangement.

She was the one changing the rules.

Lulu swallowed the knot in her throat. "Hey, look—I'm really sorry about being distant the last few days."

"No, I'm the one who needs to apologize." Preston's eyes softened as he looked down at her. "That kiss was—"

Clack.

Lulu and Preston jumped apart. Micah had walked back in the room with long pieces of trim and dropped them on the sawhorses. It was time to get to work, which was exactly what Lulu had been hoping for.

Except now she'd never know what Preston was going to say about the kiss.

"We'll talk later." Preston motioned for her to go. "We should get busy here."

"Right." Reluctantly, she joined Micah at the

sawhorses, plugging the miter saw back in and trying to concentrate on the trim beneath her blade. But somehow, despite her careful focus, she remained on constant high alert of exactly where Preston was in the room as he alternated measuring, taping and urging the girls to clean up.

She was *so* scheduling another spin class after this.

Chapter Thirteen

Preston rang the tiny bell on the counter at Oopsy Daisy. "Excuse me, ma'am?" *Ding, ding.* "I'm looking for a disgustingly spicy donut. Preferably one with chips."

"I'm sorry, what?" Across the counter, Lulu turned, wearing her logo apron over a long green sweater and leggings, a full box of donuts in her hand. Then her eyes rounded as she realized it was him and she snorted. "You're never going to let that go, are you?"

He grinned back at her. "I'll let it go when my taste buds do."

The shop was surprisingly empty for a Saturday, but he imagined the rush would be coming soon—especially with all the holiday flavors filling the display case in front of her.

"That donut wasn't meant for you." She shot him a pointed look as she folded the box flaps and then set the container on the counter. "Your *dad* loved it."

"Exactly. I thought I'd see if you had more for him." Preston took one of the stools at the counter, bracing one leg on the floor so the seat didn't spin. "He seems like he needs a pick-me-up lately."

Lulu's face fell. She leaned across the counter, her brow furrowed. "Is he okay?"

He loved that she cared so much. With all the uncertainties hovering between them, he at least knew that part for sure.

"Of course he says he's all right—and my mom backs up that claim—but I wonder." Preston lifted one shoulder in a shrug. He hadn't meant to come here and get heavy. He'd just wanted to grab his dad a treat, and, if he were honest, see Lulu. Their conversation had gotten cut off the day before on the construction site, and he really wanted to make things right between them.

And not just because his mom had another holiday double date planned.

Lulu straightened. "I don't have any more of the jalapeño potato chip cooked up, but I have been working on a new recipe for him—this time with pretzels. I'll bring them for him to try the next time I see him. Which is...when?"

He breathed a sigh of relief. She still wanted to keep hanging out, even after his faux pas the other night. "Mom actually wants to bake cookies together at my house this evening, if you're free—and not tired of baking." Funny how much he hoped she'd say yes.

And not just because his parents would be bummed if she didn't come.

"Well, I was going to put in some extra hours over at the Haven Project today, but I could come over after that."

Relief flooded through him. She was going to come over—he hadn't ruined it all. "Great. I'll help, too."

"They're really behind on the project." Lulu worked her lower lip. "I don't see how everything is going to be finished by Christmas Eve. They haven't even installed the kitchen cabinets yet."

"Have some faith." The words fled his lips before he realized how hypocritical they were. He still hadn't figured out how to pray, was constantly worried about his dad's health and yet was encouraging Lulu to hold out for a holiday miracle? But it felt right, all the same. Possible. A *lot* of things felt possible around Lulu.

Interesting how she kept bringing out the best in him.

"You're right. It'll all work out." Lulu reached inside the display case with a pair of tongs and retrieved a peppermint-dusted donut. "On the house." She quipped, "Don't worry, it's jalapeño-free."

He eagerly took a bite, the perfect combination of chocolate and peppermint melting into his mouth. He started to tell her how good it tasted but remembered how touchy she got with baking-related compliments, so he simply thanked her instead. Maybe one day she'd tell him what the deal was with all that.

Or maybe he'd finally get to know her well enough to figure it out himself.

But for that to happen, he had one more thing he *had* to say. He glanced over his shoulder to confirm they were alone in the shop, then took a deep breath. "I never got to finish my apology yesterday."

"Oh?" Lulu's eyes were suddenly darting everywhere but at him. The clock on the wall, the cash register to her right, the dried glaze on the counter between them…

"I think I overstepped that night at the gingerbread house contest." He tried to catch her gaze, interpret what she was thinking, but now she was fiddling with the fake poinsettia on the counter.

"You really did." She tugged at one of the broad leaves. "You were pretty arrogant about how well your house was built."

His eyes widened. "I was—"

Then he noticed her smile, and a thousand

pounds fled his shoulders. "I mean, it *was* a pretty sturdy house. Compared to some."

"To some," she agreed. "We won't name names, though."

"That wouldn't be gentlemanly."

"And you're a gentleman."

"I try to be." He sobered. "If I wasn't…"

"You were." She finally met his eyes fully, her quiet tone assuring him she'd gotten the gist. "You *are*. Besides, I was the one who continued this whole Operation Mistletoe plan in front of the teenagers yesterday without even asking you first."

"We were backed in a corner. I probably would have done the same." Preston blew out his breath. "This is escalating, isn't it?"

She held his gaze, nodding slowly. "It really is."

Her brown eyes seemed to hold every emotion he currently felt churning through his own heart. Concern. Hope. Confusion.

He was starting to break his own rule about not getting attached to anything—or anyone—in Tulip Mound. He squared his shoulders, determined not to make this Saturday-morning conversation any heavier than he already had. "So we're good, then?" He tapped the counter between them.

"We're good. Don't worry, I'm not backing out of our deal."

"I wasn't worried about that." He shook his head. "I was worried about us."

Surprise lit her expression. *"Us?"*

"I don't like when you're upset with me." He winced. So much for not getting heavier.

She grew quiet, which meant she wasn't denying that she had been. But something in her sudden vulnerable demeanor wasn't adding up. She was quick to forgive his slip with the brief display of PDA, but she was clearly still struggling with *something*. He waited, hoping his silence would be an invitation for her to admit the truth.

And here lately, the truth was looking more and more appealing than ever.

"*Are* you still upset with me?" he asked.

"No. I think I'm upset with myself." Her words were barely over a whisper. He leaned in close to hear better. "I know now that you and…"

"Me and who?" Preston frowned.

Lulu hesitated. "You know what? Never mind. It's silly."

"You can tell me anything." He didn't understand why Aiden, and now Lulu, kept not trusting him with their thoughts. Wasn't he being vulnerable with Lulu about his fears for his dad? He told her things.

But he hadn't told her his plans to move next summer.

He leaned back as if sucker punched. Just like

trying to discuss Aiden and his secret while carrying his own, he was keeping another one from Lulu—and being hypocritical in his expectations. It wasn't that he'd intended to keep his future plans hidden. It had just never come up, and there was initially no reason for her to know.

Now, it felt like there was.

He ran one hand over his jaw. Maybe he should go first. Get his last secret off his chest, and maybe she'd trust him with hers. Hopefully Aiden would eventually, too.

Before he could finish deciding, the chime on the door jingled and Tori, Claudia and Hayley burst into the shop. Preston abruptly sat upright, and Lulu took a quick step back from the counter. Her cheeks were flushed, but she also looked relieved.

"Your Saturday work crew is here!" Hayley announced. "We're ready to help at the Haven Project. Look, I even wore old jeans." She proudly showed off her wide-legged pants stained with something dark around the knees. "That way Claudia can't make fun of me anymore."

"*Can't* and *won't* are very different words." Claudia draped over the back of the barstool next to Preston. "Isn't that right, Teach?"

Tori stared at Preston's half-eaten donut. "Oh, is that a peppermint chocolate?"

He laughed, unable to hang on to any disappointment at the interruption. No wonder Lulu loved these teens. It was fun getting to see a side of them they never showed in the classroom. In fact, a part of him already was going to miss them when he moved to Colorado.

"It sure is. How about one for everyone?" He laid a ten-dollar bill on the counter.

Lulu shot him an approving smile, one that made him feel like he'd won a lifetime supply of donuts. Before he could analyze that too thoroughly, she broke eye contact and began pulling the treats from the case, lining them on the counter on daisy-printed napkins.

"Thanks, Teach." Claudia slapped him a high five. The others joined in with their gratitude, mouths full.

He glanced behind them at the empty shop. "Hey, where's Aiden?"

"Haven't seen him today." Hayley shrugged, pulling off a chunk of peppermint from her donut. "We usually run into him on the way here."

Hmm. Hopefully Aiden wasn't still upset about the whole mishap with the secret from yesterday. Talk about bad timing for that conversation.

And the kid still didn't realize Preston had an even bigger secret. Guilt prickled, and he quickly finished the rest of his donut. Looked like there was still one more thing he needed to make right today.

She couldn't believe she'd almost confessed about Gabrielle.

Lulu stood back as two of Mr. Settle's crew worked on laying the faux hardwood in the living room. She'd been hunting for a screwdriver so Preston could tighten the bathroom light fixture that was loose on the wall, then gotten distracted when she saw the floor was finally being put in. The relief that flooded through her at the simple sight reminded her that she really had to quit overreacting to things.

All the things. Like, why did it matter that Gabrielle and Preston used to date? She had no claim on Preston outside of Operation Mistletoe—and it wasn't like he'd lied. He had no reason to tell her about his past girlfriends, just like she'd no business telling him about her exes. Well, ex, singular, anyway.

She watched the men carefully lining up the laminate planks. Sure, it had been jolting to discover the news about Gabrielle and had provided extra insight into Preston's motivation for needing a fake date, but beyond that, it shouldn't have affected her. She'd let it get her all worked up for nothing.

Same with the Home for the Holidays progress. The floor was being installed, which meant the house was that much closer to being completed for Christmas Eve. There really wasn't any need to panic. The cabinets would be put in next, along with the hardware and the sink installation. And, at some point after that, the primer and paint—which she and all the teens could all help with. Then they could get the tiny details completed, such as getting the switch covers placed on the wall—things that wouldn't prevent the winning family from moving in but would be nice to have ready for them, all the same.

Which included actually taking the screwdriver back to Preston. Lulu took a step backward and accidentally kicked a bucket sitting on the floor behind her. The handle clanged into the side of the pail and the two men laying the flooring jerked their heads around to stare at her.

"Sorry!" She sheepishly straightened the bucket, then slipped out of the room into the kitchen. See? She gave herself plenty of reasons to be embarrassed as it was. Admitting that Gabrielle and Preston's past relationship shook her was one she didn't have to add to the naturally occurring list.

"Lulu, come quick!" Tori suddenly burst into the kitchen and grabbed her hand. "You've got to see this."

"What's going on? Did someone get hurt?" Lulu jogged after her to the front door, which was standing open. She stepped outside, frantically looking around. It'd gotten colder, and the sky was thick with snow clouds, but beyond that, she didn't see any cause for concern.

She spun around. "Tori, what did—"

"Are you okay?" Preston stood framed in the doorway, looking equally confused. "Claudia said that you—"

The door slammed shut behind him, knocking him forward a step. He gained his balance as muted giggles sounded from the foyer window. Tori's face was plastered against the smudged glass, Claudia peering over her shoulder with a wide grin. "Look up!" she called through the dirty window.

Lulu obliged. And there, dangling over her and Preston's heads, was a piece of mistletoe.

He was staring up at it, too, which gave her an up-close view of his strong jawline covered in day-old stubble. Her heart started up like one of the jackhammers a crew member had used at the groundbreaking of the project.

"Merry Christmas!" Tori hollered before breaking into another round of stifled laughter. Claudia put one hand over Tori's eyes and shot them a thumbs-up before yanking her away from the window.

"I think it's fairly safe to assume they did this." Preston looked down at Lulu, a slight grin curving the corner of his mouth.

"It's pretty cute, really." She shoved her hands into her back pockets so he wouldn't see them starting to shake. "I mean, since they think we're together and all."

"Right." Preston cleared his throat. "They don't know the truth."

"Right," Lulu echoed. "The truth." Had he stepped closer, or was she imagining things?

His cologne, deep and musky, suddenly filled her senses, until it was all she could smell. Until all she could see was his face, his eyes deep blue like the winter sky above her, and just as stormy. And all she could hear was her own heart thudding in her chest, as if someone had attached a microphone to it.

"I'm pretty sure they locked the door." Preston's voice washed over her, slightly huskier than usual. "I think we're stuck."

She was also pretty sure he hadn't checked the knob, and that fact ushered the herd of flying reindeer back into her stomach. She looked back up at the dangling green bunch over their heads, then at his questioning gaze. "It is a tradition, after all."

"A Christmas tradition," Preston agreed. "It'd be a shame to break it."

"Yeah, we wouldn't want to be grinches." She took a tiny step closer to him on the front stoop.

He closed the remaining few inches, his voice dropping to a whisper. "Definitely not." He slowly took her hand, then the other, drawing them up to his chest and pulling her in. The lightweight sweater he wore did little to mask the firmness of his form beneath her palms.

He dipped his head, and his gaze sought hers, as if asking permission. She really hoped her eyes answered with a resounding *yes*. Because if he didn't hurry up and kiss her, she wasn't sure her thudding heart would even make it to Christmas morning.

Then suddenly, he did.

His lips covered hers in a brush so gentle, she almost thought she'd missed it. Before she could open her eyes, he was back with a second kiss, one much more confident as his lips moved with hers.

The reindeer in her stomach broke into full flight.

She kissed him back, acknowledging the burst of fireworks erupting behind her closed eyes. Joy, like a slow-release bath bomb, seeped into her heart, spreading a fresh pattern of colors into places she hadn't even realized were gray.

She'd been wrong. Wrong to be jealous, wrong to worry a single iota about Gabrielle and his past, wrong to think Preston was just acting with Lulu. This kiss was *not* the work of a thespian. Or the work of a man comparing her with anyone else.

This kiss was a work of art.

Slowly, reluctantly, Preston pulled away, keeping her folded hands resting on his chest. He sounded slightly out of breath. "Lulu. This is probably not—"

"A good idea." Lulu rose on her tiptoes to meet Preston's lips more fully, and the next thing she knew, her arms broke the barricade between them and slid up around his neck. She'd never felt like this before. Not with Neal, or anyone. This kiss convinced her that all her fears were unfounded.

She *was* good enough.

Somewhere, far away, a warning bell started to break through the haze clouding her mind and heart. They weren't really alone on the front stoop. And the kids were most certainly spying.

She quickly broke away as the reindeer retreated from her stomach.

Operation Mistletoe had just gotten a lot more complicated.

Chapter Fourteen

Preston stared at the test papers in his lap, red pen tapping a rhythm on his leg as he continued reading the same paragraph over and over from his position in his recliner.

He'd kissed Lulu.

Tap tap.

Lulu had kissed him.

Tap tap.

They'd kissed each other.

Tap tap tap.

His parents would be there in about an hour for his mom's next dose of Christmas cheer—this time, in the form of cookie baking—and his attempt at getting ahead on some work had thus far failed. He'd turned on holiday music, which was playing softly in the background, and had a fire going in the electric fireplace, but even those mood-setting efforts couldn't keep his focus.

All he could think about was what would happen in the next little while when Lulu showed up at his door. She was due to arrive about the same time as his folks, though hopefully she'd come early so they could discuss that kiss.

Make that *kisses*.

Remembering them now sent his heart thudding and he stared harder at the messy handwriting before him. But it was to no avail.

After the whole mistletoe situation, Hayley's mother had pulled into the driveway to pick her up, so there was an immediate flurry of activity that kept Lulu and him separated. Then Aiden finally arrived as Hayley left, and Preston spent the next hour trying to enlist the boy's help. Aiden had done so, though silently, following him from task to task with zero conversation. Clearly, the window of opportunity Preston once had with the kid had slammed shut, and he was going to need more than a screwdriver to pry it back open. He wasn't sure which project Lulu had gotten tied up with while he'd been working with Aiden, but it had kept her in a totally different part of the house.

Or maybe she'd intended it that way.

He was equal parts nervous and eager to see her tonight—and just as equally torn about what to say. And to think he'd been worried that the forehead kiss at the contest had complicated things. Ha. *This* kiss, well… It was a league all its own. He hadn't been pretending, and if Lulu was, the woman deserved an Academy Award.

Operation Mistletoe had turned personal, and he had no idea what Lulu thought about it. Would she pull back again? Would she finally tell him what was bothering her? Did it even matter anymore?

All those questions circling his head destroyed any chance of concentrating on a high schooler's essay on World War II leadership. With a sigh of defeat, he tossed the ungraded paper on the end table and pinched the bridge of his nose. He knew better than to give this kiss too much thought, yet here he was, analyzing every detail as if there could be any other end result than one.

Because as amazing as the kiss was, he was leaving in roughly six months. Even if the job in Denver didn't pan out, he had the experience now to snag a position as a professor in another city. Going back for more with Lulu would only end in heartache for them both.

And hadn't they both had enough of that?

His cell rang, and he pulled it from his pocket. It was Jackson.

For once, the sight of his brother's name on his screen was a welcome distraction. He had to get his mind on something else. At this point, he'd talk to a telemarketer. "Hey."

"Bro." As always, Jackson sounded confident, self-assured and like the world was going exactly his way.

Preston shook off the immediate annoyance. "What's up?"

"How's Dad?"

"He's okay." He leaned back in the chair, tucking one arm behind his head. The fact that Jackson called him for an update was big. Normally, he'd be the one calling Preston to give information that he always seemed to have first. It was nice being on the info-giving side for once. "I'm surprised you haven't asked Mom."

"I did."

Oh. He cleared his throat. "And?"

"I didn't believe her. She said he was doing great, but I remember last time and how she kept trying to smooth things over." Jackson sighed. "I'd rather have the truth."

Wouldn't they all? Guilt nipped again at Preston's chest. "I think Dad is tired, but fine."

"I'm surprised Mom wanted to visit that long, honestly."

Preston bristled. "Why do you say that?"

Jackson laughed. "Come on, man. It's Tulip Mound. Once you get your Christmas tree and a few cups of cocoa, there's not much else to do."

"That's not true. We've done a lot." Preston blinked. Why was he feeling defensive over a town he was intending to leave? Probably because his brother always seemed to know everything, and this time, he was wrong. "There was also a gingerbread house contest, and Mom and Dad are coming over tonight to bake cookies. And on Christmas Eve there's a big candlelight service outside, where they'll announce the winner of the Home for the Holidays."

"The what?" Jackson's voice pitched with confusion.

"You know, the house we've been working on. That Lulu..." Preston then realized his brother didn't know anything about the Haven Project. "Never mind." He might only be a three-hour drive away, but he and his brother would forever be worlds apart.

"I see. Well, it's good you have time for all that. Work has been keeping me busy here. The company is booming, and this is normally our slower season."

"Congratulations." Preston forced the word from his mouth, reminding himself that his brother's success wasn't a threat to his own. They were in totally different industries. Educators had time off as a perk of teaching. That didn't mean his career was worth any less.

"Yeah, it's great, but hey—it must be nice to have some holiday playtime."

Preston's spine stiffened. "I'm not *playing*. I'm

helping take care of Dad. And Lulu even made him—"

"Oh, that reminds me. Listen, I know times are probably tight right now...and I'd like to help."

"Help with what?" His brother wasn't making sense.

Jackson sighed. "Come on, man, don't make this awkward. I'm offering to help."

"Dude, what are you talking about?" Preston leaned forward in his chair.

"Assist with any holiday expenses. I know Mom and Dad are paying extra medical bills right now, so they probably aren't throwing anything your way to cover all these outings Mom's coming up with. And it's Christmas."

Preston's stomach knotted into a ball. "So?"

"*So*, I thought with your being just a schoolteacher and all, you might need some financial aid."

Just a schoolteacher.

He couldn't believe Jackson. And yet, he could. This was how his brother always operated. Preston gritted his teeth, counting to ten twice before responding. "I've got it covered."

"Suit yourself." Jackson quickly said his goodbyes and got off the phone, which saved Preston the trouble of deciding whether to hang up on him.

His mom used to tell him Jackson didn't mean

those things the way he said them, but Preston was never quite sure. And the older he got, the more he figured his brother knew exactly what he was doing. Like now.

Sometimes, Preston missed the early years when they got along, when Jackson was still the annoying little brother, but the kind Preston wanted to watch out for. Before Jackson grew up and stopped needing his big brother's protection. Before he made it big and flaunted his success. Before all that drama with Gabrielle...

Preston stared at the papers waiting to be graded that were strewn around his living room and sighed. Maybe his brother thought of him as "just a schoolteacher" right now, but he'd be forced into silence next year when Preston took that professor's job in Denver.

He *had* to get that position. And if not that one, one like it.

He grabbed for his laptop and started searching job openings as his mood-setting holiday background music changed to a silly tune about a kid wanting a hippopotamus for Christmas. He could relate to the animated intensity of the singer's words. Except he didn't want a giant mammal for the holidays—all he wanted for Christmas was a little bit of respect.

Which felt just about as likely as waking up to a hippo under the tree.

* * *

Something was off.

Lulu pressed the tree-shaped cookie cutter into the flattened dough lying on Preston's kitchen counter and cast him a quick glance from the corner of her eye. He was pulling a finished batch from the oven with a buffalo-plaid oven mitt his mother had brought to "holiday up" his kitchen, and still he wore a worried frown.

She pressed her fingers between her eyes to smooth the lines she was sure were forming in response. They hadn't had a chance to talk about the kiss yet, since she'd arrived several minutes after his parents, so maybe that was the reason for the distracted air he had tonight.

Or maybe he was regretting the embrace and didn't want her here.

She laid the tree cookie on the freshly sprayed pan next to its twin and started to cut out another one. Tonight, despite his welcoming hug when she arrived and the small talk they'd made with his parents while preparing the dough, he seemed to be acting more like the Preston from before—the one she didn't really know at all. The Preston whose shirts were always perfectly ironed and whose hair was perfectly gelled and who came in weekly for a repeat order for the teachers' lounge.

Buttoned-up-and-pressed Preston, not the

candy-throwing, pun-exchanging, tree-chopping man who had shared his worries about his father and took Aiden under his wing and who had kissed her under the mistletoe.

She released a sigh. No sense jumping to conclusions until they could talk.

"Hey, Preston?"

He barely glanced her way as he set the hot tray on the wire rack next to the oven. "Yeah?"

"What do you get when you use a deer-shaped cookie cutter?"

He slid the next waiting tray into the oven and shrugged. "I'm not sure."

"A cookie *doe*."

His half smile sent her heart plummeting. He hadn't even chuckled. Something was definitely up. His parents were in the next room drinking cocoa and waiting to start decorating once the cookies cooled, so this was possibly her only chance to get to the bottom of this for the rest of the night.

She took a deep breath, then caught his hand. Unfortunately, it was the one still wearing the oven mitt, and it slid off onto the floor. "Oops. I'll get it."

"Let me."

But they both reached for it at the same time, knocking heads as they straightened.

"I'm so sorry!" Lulu clutched her forehead

with one hand and pressed against the stinging pain starting behind her eyes.

"My fault." He offered a pained smile. "I'll get it."

She perched on the barstool out of the way, her thoughts racing as embarrassment flooded her cheeks with heat. Maybe that was what was wrong tonight—Preston was realizing what he'd done earlier and was having second thoughts. He was much too put together to want to be with someone who couldn't get through a single activity without a catastrophe.

She'd arrived at his house that evening hopeful, thinking maybe she'd been right about earlier—that her assumption about what type of woman Preston wanted after hearing of his past relationship with Gabrielle wasn't accurate, after all. No one could fake a kiss like the one she and Preston had just shared. If Lulu hadn't been his type in the past, she clearly could be in the present. The kiss had proved it.

But now, watching Preston grab for the bottle of Tylenol and toss the oven mitt on the counter, she wasn't so sure.

His back to her, he braced both arms against the counter, lowered his head and took a deep breath. "I'm being a jerk."

She didn't argue, just waited.

Then he turned to face her, his expression

back to the Preston she'd come to know—and appreciate. Open. Kind. Genuine. "I'm sorry."

"It's okay. I'm sorry I can't seem to make it a week without performing a Three Stooges act." She shrugged and offered a smile, but it felt timid. She might have knocked his head, but he'd knocked her confidence.

He came to sit on the barstool next to her, spinning toward her so their knees brushed. "I don't see you that way."

She snorted. "But I know I'm too—"

"You're Goldilocks, remember?" He reached over and tucked a strand of her hair behind her ear. "Nothing *too* about it. It's just…" He took a deep breath. "We haven't gotten to talk about the kiss yet. And then my brother and I *did* talk, and I'm not handling any of the stress well."

She frowned. "Kissing me is stressful?"

"No! That's not what I meant."

She squinted at him. "Then can you say what you do mean?"

He glanced behind her toward the door separating them from his parents, then met her gaze. "I don't know how much time we have before this great holiday bake-off, but I need you to understand two things."

She nodded, heart racing. "I'm ready." Maybe. Depending on what he was going to say.

"First, and most importantly, that joke was horrible." He grinned.

She swatted his leg. *"Next."*

"Secondly..." He took her hand, rubbing one finger over the top of her knuckles. "Kissing you was probably the least stressful thing I've done in years."

Warmth crawled up her throat.

"So much so, I considered placing mistletoe all around the house tonight." He dipped his head and peered into her eyes. "Believe me?"

She squeezed his hand, knowing her face surely resembled Rudolph's nose. "I believe you."

"Which leads me to number three." His expression sobered.

Her heart hitched. "What is it?" She hoped nothing else had happened with his father. Had the doctor called and—

"I'm moving to Colorado this summer."

She pulled her hand free, the warmth immediately draining from her face. Now she just felt cold. "Colorado?" She struggled to switch gears, to transition from the fear of something being worse with Harold, to the relief that it wasn't, to the new shock of Preston...*leaving*?

"I didn't tell you before because I didn't think it mattered." He braced his hands on his knees. "But now, I think it does."

Her heart rate jumped into overdrive. "Because of the kiss."

"Well, yes, partly."

"So this has been your plan all along? Leaving Tulip Mound?" Her thoughts whirled. Nothing made sense. She'd come here tonight thinking there could possibly be a future for them, that she could be enough…and now, not only was he very much *not* offering those things, but he was also planning to move a plane ride away.

From her.

"I have an opportunity to be a professor in Denver. It's been a goal of mine since before I even came Tulip Mound—I just needed the teaching experience first to be considered."

Hope flickered, like the last ember in a campfire. "So it's not a done deal? You're not hired?"

"Not yet, but I have a great shot." He swallowed hard, looking miserable but not nearly as awful as she felt. "But if it's not in Colorado, it'll be somewhere else. I want to work at a university. I want to be somewhere that I can really make a difference."

"What about the teenagers here? They look up to you. You make a difference to them."

He opened his mouth, then closed it, but she could hear the words he wasn't speaking as clearly as if he had shouted them. *It isn't enough.*

She abruptly stood from her stool, drawing

a curtain over her heart until she could process all this later. Alone. With a bowl of homemade icing she'd eat with her finger. "Well, thanks for telling me."

"Lulu, I never meant for this to happen." His voice cracked as if he'd meant it. And he probably did. Neither of them had planned for mistletoe—neither the operation, nor the bunch of greenery hanging over the Home for the Holidays door. "My parents don't even know about my plans yet."

Ah. More secrets.

"It's fine." She returned to the tray of cookies, shuffling the cooled trees off the pan with a spatula. "You never promised anything other than helping me out with the Haven Project. And I never agreed to anything other than to help you with your parents."

He started to protest, but she silenced him by waving the spatula. "We should go back to that plan. The rest just…happened." Her tone and body language added a silent "no big deal" but her heart screamed otherwise as she continued moving cookies onto the parchment paper to decorate.

She was such a fool. The men in her life never knew what they wanted. They simply couldn't be trusted to be consistent. First her father, then Neal. Now, Preston had tried to have his donut and eat it, too, and well—that was impossible. Lulu really didn't blame him. She blamed herself.

She should have known better.

Abruptly, she dropped the spatula. "You know what? I think I need to go home. My stomach isn't feeling too hot."

"Please don't go." Preston reached toward her, but she whirled away as she untied the apron she'd worn around her waist. "I don't want things to end like this."

"They're not ending. After all, they never really started, right?" She tossed the apron on the barstool and forced a smile. "I'll see you Christmas Eve at the candlelight service. To finish our agreement." She turned away from his regretful expression. Well, she had regrets too.

He followed her toward the door. "I still owe you some Haven Project hours."

"You don't owe me anything," she responded quietly as she grabbed her purse. She just wanted to go home before the tears pressing behind her eyes escaped. She headed for the foyer. "Tell your parents I'm sorry I'm not feeling great." She reached for the doorknob, heart pounding in her ears. She was almost there. Almost to her bowl of icing.

"Hey, Lulu?"

She reluctantly turned to see Preston standing

with his hands in his pockets, a sheepish smile on his face. "Why did the girl go to the doctor after eating a cookie?"

"Ha. That one's easy." A sad smile tilted her lips. "She was feeling 'crumby.'"

The door rattled as it shut behind her.

Chapter Fifteen

Talk about feeling crummy.

Preston pushed a cinnamon ball candy into a smear of white icing on his Santa-hat-shaped cookie. None of that conversation with Lulu had gone as he'd hoped, but what did he expect? They'd kissed, and then he blurted he was moving. Of course she'd take that personally, no matter how many times he'd assured Lulu it wasn't about her. He hadn't thought it through—hadn't thought any of it through except for getting his secret off his chest. He didn't stop to consider Lulu's feelings in the big revelation, only his own.

Which made him all the more determined to protect his dad for as long as possible. It'd be selfish to do anything differently at this point. They'd come so far. If Lulu was still willing to continue with Operation Mistletoe through Christmas, then they'd have to just figure it out.

He couldn't keep letting people down.

Preston piped another lining of white icing onto the next Santa hat.

Besides, there was no reason he and Lulu wouldn't still be good friends, even after he moved. Friends sometimes kissed and stayed just friends, right?

Right. And Rudolph really flew Santa's sleigh.

He dropped the icing tube with a groan and pressed his fingers against his temples. He should call her, but his instinct warned him she needed space for a while first.

Maybe just a text...

Just as he reached for his phone, his mother pushed into the kitchen, carrying two mugs. "I'm sorry Lulu wasn't feeling well." She dumped the remains of hot chocolate into the sink.

Preston couldn't help but notice his father's mug had barely been drunk. Dad must not be feeling too great tonight, either—though his ailment was legit. Preston didn't blame Lulu for bailing, though.

He'd driven her to it, with his selfishness.

"She said she was sorry to have to leave." Preston pushed the tube of icing away from him, hoping his mom would leave it at that.

"I'm sure we'll see her in a few days. I can't believe Christmas is so soon!" Mom leaned against the counter, pausing to snag a tree cookie decorated with sprinkles. She took a tiny bite. "Speaking of... What are you giving Lulu?"

So far, he was pretty sure all he'd given her was a headache. "I haven't gotten her anything yet."

"Preston!" Mom straightened abruptly and pointed at him with her cookie. "What are you waiting for? The stores will be picked over. You need to go get her something special." She looked like she expected him to grab his wallet and his car keys right then.

"Relax, I've got it covered." Covered as in, he had no idea what to give her for Christmas, and hadn't realized until that very moment it would be expected. And not just because his parents would be watching, but because their friendship had reached that level by now even without his folks in the picture. He should get her something. He *wanted* to get her something. Ideally, something that would apologize for his actions the last few days, for complicating this whole charade so completely.

But what?

"If you need ideas..." His mom's voice trailed off and she crooked her finger at him. "Follow me."

He reluctantly pushed back from the island and followed his mom to her purse, which was sitting in the living room on the coffee table.

His father snoozed in the recliner, the TV softly playing the ends of an animated Christmas movie. The scene should have been cozy, but all it did was fill Preston with a sense of unease. To anyone else, it looked like a contented man relaxing after a fun evening. But Preston knew the truth.

Nothing was really as it appeared this holiday, was it?

Mom pulled a container of mints, then a package of tissues, from her bag.

Preston raised his eyebrows. "I'm not really sure that conveys the right message, Mom."

"Hush. I'm getting there." She finally unburdened her purse enough to find the zipper compartment she'd been searching for and removed a velvet pouch.

A jewelry pouch.

Oh, no.

Mom set her purse down, then motioned for Preston to sit on the couch with her. Numbly, he complied.

"Here." She pulled open the gold ties on the little navy bag and motioned for him to hold his hands out. He obliged, and she dropped something hard and cold into his cupped palms. His shoulders tensed before he even opened his fingers. A ring.

An heirloom diamond ring.

Her voice gentled. "Maybe this is what you need to give Lulu this year?"

He stared at the glistening diamond. It wasn't big enough to be obnoxious, but it was impressive—oval cut, surrounded by tiny yellow topaz gemstones.

Lulu's favorite color.

For a moment, he imagined what it would be like to truly be in a relationship with Lulu. To have her come over, not because of a prearranged business transaction, but because she simply wanted to. To have food fights and swing hammers and share mistletoe kisses without the shadow of a charade hanging over them.

He imagined what it would be like to get down on one knee and slip this very ring onto Lulu's finger. To spend a future with her surrounded by donuts and teenagers and construction projects.

It sounded…nice. Comfortable. And not in the stretched-out-old-sweater kind of way, but in the "fits just right" way.

But he wasn't ready to give up his dream job. He couldn't be the right man for Lulu when he still wasn't who he needed to be for himself. He needed that career upgrade, that position in Denver. Needed the validation that came with it, before he'd be good enough for anyone like Lulu.

"This ring was my grandmother's." Mom smiled, clearly oblivious to his inner turmoil.

"You know I'm an only child, as was my mother, so she never had a son to pass it on to. It's still here in the family, waiting for a recipient."

The fact that she'd chosen to offer it to him instead of Jackson meant more than she'd ever know. A rush of warmth filled his chest, momentarily replacing the guilt of her offering it at all when he was very much single. As the oldest son, Preston *should* have the first shot with it. But that wasn't typically how things worked in their family.

He turned the ring gently in his hands, studying the way the diamond caught the canned lighting above them. The question niggled at his mind, relentless, and he had to know for sure. "Why didn't you give it to Jackson?"

"Well, I tried. But he wanted to pick out his own ring for Gabrielle." Mom shrugged, but a mist of hurt shone in her eyes.

He felt the same hurt pressing in the back of his throat. "I see." Jackson, being the best, the first, the chosen, once again. He hated this rivalry that he often wondered if his brother even noticed or felt it, too. He didn't want to be better than Jackson, he just wanted to be on the same level. Wanted to have the type of friendship they had when they were younger, before growing up...before Gabrielle...complicated everything.

And most of all, he just wanted his brother to quit rubbing his favorite status in Preston's face.

"He had need of it sooner." Mom touched his knee. "That was all." She offered a little shrug. "I think both of you have found lovely women, and I don't care which of them wear this ring so long as it stays in the family. It's more important to me that you're in thriving, healthy relationships."

Thriving and healthy—definitely not his situation. The guilt returned. Not only had he and Lulu been pretending this whole time, but then he'd kissed her and immediately told her he was moving away. Big jerk move. He'd dismissed what that kiss meant without even giving her—or them—a chance. He tried to sweep it under the proverbial rug and then, despite her obvious hurt, had just wanted to keep Operation Mistletoe chugging along like nothing had happened. Like he hadn't been the one to sabotage the whole operation in the first place.

Nothing healthy about that. Their friendship deserved better. *Lulu* deserved better. Maybe that kiss had been mutual, but Operation Mistletoe had been his idea.

This was his fault.

Now Lulu would never trust him enough to see things differently—and he wouldn't deserve it if she did. It was better for everyone if he started over in Denver.

After all, wasn't the right person at the wrong time still the wrong person?

Preston blew out a slow breath, wishing he could pray for guidance. Wishing he didn't feel so distant with God, along with everyone else. He glanced at his father, who snored lightly in his sleep, and felt like the weight of the universe balanced directly on his shoulders. The last thing he wanted to do was stress his dad out with the truth, but the fact that Preston was holding a diamond ring confirmed this had all gone way too far.

There was no time for more prayers to bounce off the ceiling. He knew what he had to do.

He briefly closed his fingers over the ring, then held his hand out toward his mother. "Thanks, Mom. But I don't think this is the right move."

The right move was coming clean. Even though Jackson would have a field day with that information and would never let Preston live it down, he had to do it.

But he couldn't tell his parents the whole story without talking to Lulu first. She was too invested in this for him to bombard her like that. He refused to do anything else she might consider hurtful. As soon as he could, he'd let her know the jig was up, and then she'd be free to go about her holiday exactly as she wished—likely without him.

A thought that brought much more disappointment than relief. As complicated as this had gotten, he wasn't ready for Operation Mistletoe to be over.

"If it's too soon, that's fine. But you keep it." Mom held up both hands, refusing to take the ring back. "The right time will come sooner or later." She smiled knowingly. "I've seen the way you look at Lulu. It won't be long."

"What do you mean, *gone*?"

Lulu squeezed her eyes shut, hoping that when she opened them, the progress on the Home for the Holidays would be further along. The cabinets would finally be installed, the floors would be finished and the walls would be painted. Then all she'd have to do is screw in a few outlet covers and *voila*. A home completed for a family in need.

A family very much like her own growing up.

But when she opened her eyes to the partially completed rooms, nothing had changed, including Aiden's nervous gaze meeting her own.

"The crew is gone." He shrugged. "I got here this morning to help, but there was only one painter. He spoke mostly Spanish, so we kind of played charades for a minute trying to talk, then he finally showed me a text message from Mr. Settle. He canceled the painter because the kitchen isn't done yet like it was supposed to be, because he had to send his crew last night to do emergency storm relief in Topeka."

The most words she'd ever heard Aiden speak at one time, and it was bad news. Lulu groaned. She'd heard of the ice storm prediction threatening the midpart of the state the other day but dismissed it since it was so far west of Tulip Mound. They'd only gotten a light dusting of snow and a slight drop in temperature, and it'd never crossed her mind again. Of course, she felt sympathy for those affected, but at the same time, her own past twenty-four hours had been a blizzard in itself.

After leaving Preston's house last night, she'd gone straight to bed, her stomach tied in knots of regret and remorse. She'd allowed herself to catch feelings for him, despite knowing better, and until she could unravel them, it was better to just stay out of Preston's sight. She'd avoided him in church that morning, stopping to talk to his parents, then escaping to volunteer in the youth service so she wouldn't have to sit with Preston.

She'd wanted to, though.

She wanted to claim a spot on the pew between him and Harold and belt out a hymn of adoration in the Christmas season. Wanted to gently touch

Harold's shoulder and pray for healing during the invitational message. Instead, she'd prayed for him—and for her cracked heart—while dancing to choreographed worship music alongside a crowd of teenagers and listening to a youth-targeted sermon on advent.

It'd done her good to remember the real meaning of Christmas, to realign her focus back on Jesus, the God-child in the manger. But that had also fueled her desire to get this Home for the Holidays finished, because while fake dating certainly was not the reason for the season, providing for those in need very much was. She needed something to pour herself into while she processed her disappointment with Preston, and now, she couldn't do that, either.

Everything was at a standstill—buckets abandoned, wiring exposed, tiles half-laid—forcing her to look much too clearly at her own heart and expectations. And she didn't like what she saw. Didn't like how far she apparently *hadn't* come since her breakup with Neal. She thought she was healed. Thought she'd forgiven her wayward father and her selfish ex-fiancé and had moved into a place of contentment.

But she'd only been masking it with spin classes and donut recipes and miter saws.

Now she had nothing else to distract her, and the truth was not very merry.

"We should probably go, too, huh?" Aiden watched her carefully, and she could only imagine what her face must look like.

"Right…" She shook her head to clear it. "Sorry, I zoned out. I'll just make sure everything is locked up."

Aiden shuffled his feet. "You seem upset. Why don't you head out, and I'll make sure all the windows and doors are shut instead? You could probably use a break."

She gave him an appreciative gaze. He really was a sweet kid, even though he and Preston hadn't been getting along too well the last few days. But then again, Preston and she hadn't been, either.

"Thank you. That sounds great." She told the teen goodbye and headed for her car, which was parked on the street a few houses down to save room for the work trucks she'd assumed were coming.

The reminder that they weren't coming—that no one was coming, and that Christmas Eve was in three days—sank her heart once again. And not just because she needed the distraction, but because now, a low-income family wouldn't have the amazing Christmas gift they deserved.

It wasn't fair.

She buckled her seat belt, casting one last look at the Home for the Holidays project. She and the other volunteers could paint and do a lot of finishing touches, but they couldn't finish the flooring or install cabinets and sinks. There were still too many tasks left that required certified professionals, and with Micah's crew in Topeka for who knew how long, it simply wasn't going to happen in time. She had to accept that.

Had to accept a lot of things.

A shadow crossed the construction site, and Lulu squinted down the street. It was just Aiden, finally leaving. But why was he coming from around the back of the house? And why did he have a bulging backpack? He hadn't had that on while they were talking. She snorted. Or maybe he had. She'd not exactly been in the best frame of mind while talking to the poor guy.

Besides, he'd come prepared to work for the day. It was probably full of water bottles and snacks, or an extra hoodie.

She shifted her car into Drive, debating if she should go home or go straight to Oopsy Daisy. The shop was closed on Sundays, but she could pour her woes into a new recipe or bake a surprise batch of donuts for the teens.

But she was still fooling herself. All she really wanted to do was go find Preston, cry on his shoulder and hang out and play board games with Harold and Susie. She wanted to smile at the way Susie helicopter-hovered over her husband and hide her laugh at the teasing faces Harold made behind her back. She wanted to drink decaf coffee and make goofy puns with Preston.

She wanted it all to be real instead of fake.

Then she sucked in her breath. *That was it.*

Lulu pressed down on the gas pedal and turned left instead of right at the stop sign, away from Oopsy Daisy. Her heart rate accelerated just as fast.

She knew who could help.

Chapter Sixteen

Lulu searched the hat-wearing, scarf-draped heads and shoulders of the crowd in front of her as she wove her way through the portable booths of the Christmas Market. After finding Preston's house dark and his car gone from the driveway, she'd texted him and discovered he'd taken his parents Christmas shopping.

She was sure he was wondering about her vague and slightly cryptic "I'll be right there, we need to talk" response—their first communication since she'd suddenly left his house the night before. He'd probably assumed she wanted to talk about the Colorado thing, or the mistletoe thing, but it was most definitely neither.

The Haven Project was all she cared about right now.

She craned her head to see around the maze of pom-pom beanies and Santa hats blocking her view and was almost ready to give up and text him again when she spotted him.

There. By the hot chocolate booth.

Lulu started to cut across the crowd toward Preston, narrowly missing a collision with a mother clutching the hands of twin boys. She stopped and waited while a frazzled-looking father chased after the trio, pulling a red wagon laden with shopping bags. Then two teenagers Lulu recognized from the high school paraded past next, texting as they walked, followed by Gretchen—resident foster mom and founder of the Tulip House. Finally, she seized the break in the crowd and darted to Preston's side.

Now that she was this close, her nerves jumped into full alert. He had to agree to this... he just had to.

She swallowed hard before tapping his shoulder. "Hi."

"Hey! You made it." He turned with a smile, offering a cup of hot chocolate. Several shopping bags dangled from the crook of his arm. "Here, this one's for you."

He'd gotten her a drink—even after she'd bailed so quickly last night and had been radio silent until her panicked text fifteen minutes ago.

Chagrined, she took the warm to-go cup covered in a cardboard sleeve. "Thank you."

"Mom and Dad are somewhere around here."

Preston scanned the crowd behind her, and for a moment, Lulu was sure it was to avoid looking her directly in the eye. But then he did, and the royal blue Henley he wore practically electrified his gaze.

She fought the urge to take a step back, away from his proximity and cologne and Preston-ness. "I'm sure I'll find them next."

"They'll want to see you."

Lulu offered a rueful shrug. "And make sure I'm okay?"

"Something like that." Preston's smile sobered.

She drew a deep breath. "I'm sorry I ran out so quickly last night. I just…"

"It's all right." Preston touched her arm, then quickly dropped his hand. But she still felt the lingering remains of his touch, warmer than the mug of chocolate in her grip.

He cleared his throat. "Totally understandable after the bomb I dropped on you. I'm sorry for telling you like that. At the time, it seemed like the right thing to do, but I could have done it better."

Maybe. But she really didn't want to get into that. And at the end of the day, it didn't matter. Couldn't matter.

Because he was still leaving.

"That's actually not what I came to talk to you

about." She shook her head. "But we do need to talk."

"This sounds serious." Preston touched her elbow again, steering her away from the beverage stand and to a slightly less crowded corner of the town square. Across the way, a line of squirming kids had formed near the gazebo to see Santa—make that Clyde—and his duo of elves in striped leggings.

"It is serious." Lulu took a fortifying sip of cocoa, then a deep breath. "The Haven Project got put on hold. Micah's crew were dispatched to do emergency storm repair in Topeka."

"Oh, man." Concern crested Preston's face. "That's terrible. That must have been a much bigger storm than I initially heard about."

Relief that he agreed it was serious flooded Lulu's body. "I know. Now the Home for the Holidays won't be ready by Christmas Eve for the big reveal. There are too many projects we're still waiting to have professionally installed for the volunteers to finish the workload alone."

"Is there another local organization that can take this on?"

Lulu sighed. "Unfortunately no. I got Micah on the phone on the way over, and he said he's already called around, but couldn't find anyone. It's too last-minute. No one is prepared, especially with this being a pro bono project."

Preston took a swig from his cup. "That's a real shame."

"But maybe there's a crew that's *not* local."

He dipped his chin toward her. "You mean, a company from out of town is coming to help?"

"They might." Lulu took a deep breath, fiddling with the ends of her yellow scarf. "If you call them." She risked a peek into his eyes.

Confusion created a fog, then slowly dissipated as his eyebrows rose higher on his forehead. "You want me to ask Jackson?"

She nodded, but he was already shaking his head. Panic pressed against her chest. This was their only chance. "It's for a good cause."

His lips formed a thin line. "You don't understand what you're asking."

"No, *you* don't understand what you're refusing." She gestured to the market happening around them. "This is a big deal for the community. A family needs this home. How can you refuse to do your part to make that happen?"

"I *have* done my part." Preston's voice, while it didn't grow louder, grew firmer. "I've volunteered as much as possible over my entire winter break—with intentions to do more as soon as there's something for me to do."

"But there is something for you to do. Don't you see?" Lulu swallowed back the frustration building in her throat.

"I see what you're saying." He stepped closer, and she fought the contradicting urge to step away…and fall into his embrace. She missed the nearness she'd grown accustomed to over the past few weeks, missed having the "right" to sit close and brush his shoulder with her own, missed having him lean in and whisper to her or joke. She missed *that* Preston.

But this Preston…the one hesitant to help, wasn't the man she thought he was.

Although to that point…hadn't *that* Preston just been pretending in front of his family?

She stepped away. Maybe she really didn't know him at all.

His arm that had been reaching for her slowly lowered to his side. "What I don't see is the big rush. The project will get completed. It's not like Jackson is the only solution."

She crossed her arms over her chest, splattering hot chocolate on her jacket and not even caring. "He's the only solution to having it done for Christmas Eve on Tuesday."

Preston blew out his breath as he gestured with a shopping bag. "Even that's a long shot. I don't know his production schedule."

"And you won't…if you don't ask." She hugged herself tightly, hating the tears burning relentlessly behind her eyes. His relationship with Jackson wasn't ideal, but he should be able to put aside petty differences for a good cause. This was so important. Why couldn't he see that? Without his help, a family in need would spend Christmas without a home and, worst of all, without hope.

She knew.

She'd been there.

He inched a step closer, lowering both his head and his voice. "I can't ask him right now. It's the worst timing possible."

"Worse than a family not getting a home for Christmas?" She heard the sharpness in her tone but couldn't find a way to dull the knife. Her own hurt bled over everything.

His expression drew serious. "Lulu, there's something I haven't told you…"

She briefly closed her eyes. Great. Was Colorado not far enough away? Was he moving to Australia, instead?

Clyde's booming *ho ho ho* echoed across the yard, mixing with the sounds of giggling kids, chattering adults and the faint strains of Christmas carols playing from a nearby speaker. The clash of their tense conversation against the merry moments only added heaviness to her weary heart. She opened her eyes. "What is it?"

"I needed to talk to you tonight, too." He shifted his shopping bags to his other arm and sighed. "We're going to have to tell my parents the truth."

She stiffened. "What? Why?"

"It's time. This has gotten way out of control."

"Wait." She held up one hand to stop whatever he was going to say next. Nothing about this Christmas was going the way it was supposed to. She missed her mom. She missed the connection she thought she'd had with Preston. And now, he was going to take Harold and Susie away from her, too? They'd been the best part of this entire charade, and now that he was over it...over *her*...he was going to pull the plug?

Rejection came in many forms, and she was familiar with them all.

She sniffed, desperate for a reason, *any* reason other than the one she was forming on her own. "What about your dad's health? Is he better?" That would be a good reason. Maybe the only one.

"Nothing's changed that I know of." Preston tossed his cup into a nearby trash can, seemingly unable to meet her eyes. "Although I don't know that they'd tell me if it had."

"Then why risk it? Wasn't the whole point in doing this to protect his health?"

"Like I said, it's gotten out of control."

Lulu snorted. "I don't see how a few more days will make any difference. Can't we just—"

"No, we can't." He ran his hand over his hair, stress creasing his brow. "Can you trust me on this?"

"*Trust* you?" She reared back, trying to rein in her frustration as a strolling couple cast them curious looks. "No. And why should I? You're not who I thought you were."

A shadow crossed his face. "Because I'm not calling Jackson to come save the day?"

"That, and because you're making up the rules as you go along." The tears she'd been fighting for the past ten minutes pressed dangerously close to the surface. "You begged me to do this whole thing in the first place, and now you're changing everything all at once." It was too much.

But wasn't that always the theme of her life? There was nothing Goldilocks about her—or any of this.

Barely restrained frustration brewed in his eyes. "I need you to understand this is for the best, Lulu."

"Well, there are things I wish you could understand, too, but I guess neither of us are getting that wish for Christmas."

"Fine." His lips pressed together as he shifted his shopping bags to his other hand. "You really want to know why?" He reached inside the fold of his jacket.

"Yes! Why do we have to stop pretending now? We're this close to the finish line. Christmas Eve is only a few days away. Your parents will be going home soon and won't have to know that we were never really together—"

A ring appeared in her face. "*That's* why."

Her breath caught in her throat, along with her pride. Her heart began a slow descent to her toes. "That's a diamond ring."

"My family heirloom wedding ring, to be exact. Jackson didn't want it." Clenching his jaw, Preston put the ring carefully back into his pocket. "Believe me now when I say things are out of control?"

"Well, I for one sure do."

A feminine voice sounded behind Lulu. Her pulse thundered. Even without turning, even without acknowledging the color draining from Preston's voice, she knew.

Susie.

Lulu's sinking heart hit rock bottom, and she slowly spun to face the music. But she wasn't prepared for Harold to be standing beside his wife, hurt radiating off his drawn expression as he stared at them both.

"What exactly is going on here?" Then his face crumbled, and he sagged against Susie before crashing to the ground in a heap.

Chapter Seventeen

"That was a very exciting shopping trip." Mom sat down across from Preston at his dining room table and slid a mug of coffee toward him. "Don't worry. It's not decaf."

He took a sip, but the warm liquid did little to comfort him. Guilt assaulted the raw places inside, and he took a deep breath. "Mom, I—"

She held up one hand. "Let's wait for your father." Her tone, the same one she used when he went through a stage of forgetting to take his muddy boots off as a kid, left little room for arguing.

Preston picked up a leftover tree cookie from their recent baking extravaganza and numbly took a bite of an iced branch. Had that just been yesterday? The kiss… his announcement to Lulu about moving. Then the Christmas market, their big fight.

Lulu was right. Things *were* changing quickly, but not all of that was directly his fault.

Something nudged him then, deeper than guilt. Something more like conviction. He swallowed. He really should pray. For his dad's health. For his and Lulu's...whatever they were. For this awkward conversation he was about to have.

But why would God want to hear from him after everything he'd messed up? After all the ways he'd failed?

A few tense moments later, Dad ambled into the dining room, having swapped his jeans for sweatpants. After his father had nearly fainted at the market, Preston insisted his parents stay the night with him, instead of being alone at the inn, and had swung by the Hummingbird to grab their essentials before coming home. Harold felt confident low blood sugar had made him feel dizzy at the market and he would feel better after getting a snack.

So far, his theory proved to be true—thanks to Mom's lavish spread of cookies, cheese and crackers—but Preston found it hard to relax, just the same. The shock his father experienced had to have contributed to his episode.

"Is Lulu okay?" Dad settled into the chair at the head of the table, then took the mug Mom handed him. He stared into its depths. "This is decaf, isn't it?"

"It is what you believe it to be." She winked at Preston, and his shoulders relaxed a notch. She must not be that mad if she was joking around.

Which meant she was probably more disappointed in him than angry, which was far worse.

A fresh wave of regret washed over him until he thought he'd drown in remorse. If Lulu's face had been any indication when she'd realized his parents had heard the end of their conversation, then she felt the exact same. After choking out a teary apology to his parents, she'd pushed past Preston and disappeared into the throng of people waiting to see Santa. And, apparently, had set her phone to Do Not Disturb.

What a night. How could Lulu beg him to ask Jackson to come play hero? After everything they'd been through, after all she'd seen regarding his brother, she still expected Preston to ask him to save the day? And on the heels of this truth bomb over his and Lulu's fake relationship. Jackson would never let him live it down. Preston's stomach hurt just thinking about it. He would have zero dignity left if he made that call.

But first things first. It was his turn to say he was sorry to his parents.

He laid both hands on the tabletop. "I really need to apologize to you both."

"I'm more worried about Lulu than I am about hearing you admit your dumb idea was dumb." Dad took a slow sip of his coffee, the twinkle in his eyes loosening the tense knot in Preston's stomach. "Why'd you do it, anyway?"

"That's what I'm wondering." Mom lifted her eyes to Preston. "I know I've hinted about settling down a time or two, but was it necessary to *pretend* to have a girlfriend?"

He leaned across the table. "Mom, you know I love you, but it wasn't just 'a few times.' You set me up on blind dates with half a dozen women in a single year. Most of which you arranged before asking me."

She waved one hand. "I wasn't as bad as all that."

He leveled his gaze. "You once dropped an apple on the grocery store floor so it would roll next to an attractive woman—and made me go get it."

Dad sputtered, nearly spraying his coffee. "*Susan!* You did not."

His mom sat up straighter in her chair. "Okay, fine. I'm guilty. But I'm also guilty of wanting my sons to be happy. Did anyone ever think of that?"

Preston wrapped his hands around his mug. "To be fair, this charade wasn't just about you, Mom." He hesitated—but it was now or never. "It was also about Jackson."

"I wondered." Harold nodded. "That whole debacle with Gabrielle…"

"It wasn't a *debacle*," Mom corrected. "It all worked out the way it was supposed to."

"I agree. Gabrielle and I were never right for each." Preston pulled the ring from his pocket and gently laid it on the middle of the table. The yellow gemstones shimmered in the over-head light. "But that doesn't change the fact my younger brother married my ex-girlfriend, and I'm still single."

Mom shifted in her chair. "Well, when you put it that way…"

"Jackson and I haven't been on good terms for a while now, and not just because of Gabrielle."

"I knew something was off between you boys." His mother casually reached for a cracker from the tray between them. "I thought you'd be happy for him."

Preston sighed. "Maybe you haven't noticed how Jackson rubs things in my face?"

"I think Preston has a point." Dad held up one hand, and both Preston and his mother looked at him in surprise.

"What do you mean?" his mom asked with a frown.

"I saw the way you and Jackson interacted at dinner and at the tree farm. It seemed to go be-yond brotherly pestering." Dad shrugged. "But no one asked my opinion, so I didn't give it. You're both adults now."

"Maybe Jackson has his moments, but that hardly merits faking an entire relationship." Mom pointed at Preston with her cracker. "I still don't understand that part."

"Look, this whole thing got carried away faster than we meant for it to." He ran his finger around the handle of his mug, unable to look either of them in the eye as he filled them in on the auction and bidding on Lulu—his whole plan.

"I promise, we were going to tell you the truth after dinner that night, but then you made the announcement about Dad's cancer, and I didn't want to do anything to stress him out like last time." He shrugged. "We lost our window."

Dad cleared his throat. "Or... Maybe you didn't really want it."

"What do you mean?" Preston jerked his gaze to meet his dad.

His father nudged the ring closer toward to Preston. "I mean, I wouldn't be so quick to give this back to us."

Across the table, Mom smiled and tried to hide it behind her coffee mug.

Preston looked back and forth between them, feeling like he'd missed a large portion of the conversation. "What are you two talking about? Lulu and I aren't even really dating."

"Not now. But..." His father looked way too confident for a man in sweatpants drinking decaf coffee at nine o'clock at night.

"We've seen the way you look at her—and the way she looks at you." Mom scooted the ring toward Preston until it brushed against his knuckles. "I don't think it was all fake, son."

He frowned, letting the shift in words and tone soak in. "So you're not mad?"

"I was hurt at first." His mother laid a cube of cheese carefully on top of her cracker, her words as methodical as her actions. "But I don't blame you for wanting to protect your father's health."

Dad snorted. "I'm not an invalid."

His mother ignored him and continued. "I also hadn't realized how upset your brother made you. That's something we all need to work on, as a family. You know your father and I love you boys equally."

Dad's voice grew gravelly. "And we're proud of you both. Business owner, teacher, president, whatever. It's all the same to us."

His throat tightened. He'd needed to hear that for too long, but looking across the table at his father, Preston realized he'd never considered his parents might be pleased with him just as he was. In his quest to constantly save face with his brother, Preston had made assumptions rather than communicate.

Some of the very things he was upset at his family for doing to him.

"Personally, I'm glad you bid on Lulu and we got to meet her." Mom crunched into her cheese-and-cracker combo.

A bit of the weight lifted from his shoulders at her declaration, but Preston still felt guilty. Like he should pray. Confess. Maybe that was why he felt so blocked lately in church—all the mis-truths and misleading. It wasn't honest.

He swallowed. "You're glad…even if it was all based on a lie?"

His mom tilted her head, her light brown hair brushing across the shoulders of her Christmas sweater. "Is it really a lie if it becomes true?"

Her words resonated long after they'd cleaned up the snack tray and all headed for bed, his parents to the guest room and he to his. His feelings for Lulu had become true. He couldn't deny it anymore. The kiss had proved what he'd already known by spending so much time with this warm, quirky, generous, adorably awkward woman these last few weeks.

He flipped his pillow over, his heart racing. Colorado was still a complication. But he hadn't even given him and Lulu a chance to really be together, to let their relationship grow and see where it led. Maybe she'd consider long distance. Plus, the new job was still six months away.

The future was a big what-if, but he'd rather have the question marks be before him than behind him. Leaving next summer for a new job without ever seeing what might truly develop with Lulu would be a question that could haunt him for years to come.

He sat up abruptly in bed, typing and then deleting a dozen text messages to Lulu, before burying his face back in his pillow with a sigh. All of this was too important to text, and her phone was still obviously set to Do Not Disturb. Who knew when she'd even read them.

Besides, in his gut, he knew there was something he needed to do first. For Lulu. And for this whole town he was coming to love, despite every effort not to.

He blew out a quick breath, prayed a prayer that finally went all the way through the ceiling and didn't bounce back…and dialed his brother's number.

Chapter Eighteen

Lulu couldn't put off the inevitable any longer—she was going to have to read her texts.

She tucked the boxes of leftover donuts under her arm as she locked the door of Oopsy Daisy behind her, feeling her phone vibrate once again in her pocket. She'd finally turned it off Do Not Disturb that afternoon but hadn't made time to glance through the dozen or more texts she saw in her notifications.

She'd made way too many donuts that day, stress-baking up a storm, and even experimented with two new flavors for Harold. But no amount of mixing, frying and icing could get the memory of the sweet man's disappointed face out of her mind.

The first male figure in her life who'd seemed to truly like her and accept her as she was, and she'd crushed him.

She let out a ragged sigh, hating the niggling guilt that racked through her. She could try to blame Preston for everything, but at the end of the day, she'd gone along with this charade just as he had. She'd contributed to the mistruths that hurt his parents, and they hadn't deserved that. Even if her and Preston's motive had been a good one initially, the truth was always better. Hadn't she learned that by this point in her life?

Apparently not, because she also hadn't told Preston the *why* behind the Haven Project being so important to her. He had no idea she'd personally experienced the need for such a generous community gift.

And she didn't want to tell him because those years of her life still embarrassed her.

She'd already lost any chance of a relationship with Preston. She didn't want to lose her dignity, too. If he reacted the same way Neal had when he found out about Lulu's childhood, well—she couldn't bear it. She'd rather things end with Preston as they were, with a memory of a good friendship and an even better kiss, than have him look at her with pity. To have him hold her up to the Gabrielles of the world and come up short.

She shuffled the donut boxes in her arms as she headed for her car. Everything had turned so bad, so fast. How had she gone from having a faux family to spend Christmas with to facing a whole day alone with her regrets?

Footsteps sounded behind her, and she turned.

"Lulu, come quick!" Claudia was jogging up the sidewalk, her long-sleeved T-shirt featuring a rock band of reindeer wielding microphones. "I've been texting you." She breathed dramatically, as if the jog had taken the last of her youthful energy.

"I'm sorry, Claudia, I've been busy. I haven't even looked at my phone." Mostly because she hadn't been ready to deal with the inevitable. Lulu slid the boxes of leftover donuts into her back seat. "I've got to take these to the shelter."

"That's fine. We just need to make a stop first." The teen walked purposefully around to the passenger side and got in, buckling her seat belt before Lulu could respond.

She could protest, but it would be futile. Lulu shut the back car door, then slid in the front and cranked the engine. "Where to?" She began to merge onto the street.

"Haven Project."

She stomped the brake. "Why?" That was literally the last place she wanted to be. Didn't want to be reminded of the project's failure. Of the site of her first—and likely only—kiss with Preston.

"Just trust me. Go!" Claudia pumped her fist in the air like they were in a high-speed chase.

Sighing in resignation, Lulu dutifully drove toward Fern Avenue, though she purposefully drove about five under the speed limit. Her phone continued to buzz in her pocket, but she legitimately couldn't check it now.

They pulled onto the all-too-familiar street, and she parked the car two houses down, behind a large, paneled van. She didn't want to get too close to the property until she knew what Claudia was up to. "What are we doing here?"

The teen was already getting out of the car, a big smile on her face. "Look." She pointed.

Lulu climbed out, stepped up on the floor of her car for a better view and peered around the van...at a flurry of activity. She gasped. Workers filed in and out of the house like ants, some wearing white painter's jumpsuits, while others toted boxes of flooring and hitched up sagging tool belts. Two men carefully carried an appliance through the front door. "Was that the kitchen sink?"

"You better believe it." Claudia laughed. "It's happening! I haven't seen this many workers onsite since I first started helping."

Lulu hadn't, either. Had Micah taken pity on them and sent the crew back? But what about Topeka... No. He wouldn't do that. She frowned as she studied the faces of the passing crew. "I don't recognize any of them."

"Of course not. Aiden told me this crew is from Nebraska." Claudia could mimic Hayley's "duh" tone a little too well, but right now, Lulu didn't care.

"Nebraska?" she repeated.

Claudia crossed her arms over her chest and talked dramatically slower. "You know…that big state to the north of us? *Ne-bras-ka.*"

"I know where it is. I just don't understand what…" Her voice trailed off. Had Preston talked to his brother after all? But he'd been so adamant against it. Maybe it was his parents. Surely he told them, after their big argument. That had to be it. This seemed like just the thing that Susie would call Jackson about, without hesitation.

Lulu's phone buzzed again from her back pocket, and as she reached to grab her vibrating cell, her foot slipped from the edge of the floorboard. She grabbed for the top of the open car door to catch herself, but it was too late. Her ankle rolled and she twisted as she went down…

And landed hard on the asphalt street.

Preston eagerly climbed the hill to the Haven Project, grateful for the buzz of activity happening around him. Lulu was going to be so happy when she saw it, and that thought lifted his spirits. She still hadn't answered his texts, but he was hoping to find her here, hoping to catch her smile as she realized there was hope for the Christmas Eve home reveal tomorrow night after all.

He owed this to her, after everything he'd put her through. Lulu had been right—he was being selfish by refusing to ask Jackson to help. And as Preston had already learned with this whole charade with his parents, doing the wrong thing with a good motive still accomplished more harm than good. Maybe his personal reason for wanting to exclude Jackson from the picture was understandable, but the end result—a family not getting a home for Christmas—was far worse than any brotherly feud. His mom was right, too. They needed to deal with this as a family and stop pretending the tension didn't exist.

Though to his credit, Jackson hadn't wasted any time securing a crew from his Nebraska branch and having them commute the nearly three hours to Tulip Mound. It was an expensive decision rushing a team over at the crack of dawn at the start of a workweek, but his brother said he could spare them for a few days "for a good cause."

"Well, well, well." Jackson grinned as he strode out of the house to meet Preston, a steel clipboard in hand. "Did you bring my cape?"

And some things never changed.

Preston gritted his teeth, then held out his hand to shake his brother's, ignoring the superhero remark. "I really appreciate this."

"No biggie. It's a tax write-off." Jackson shook his hand, then shrugged. "Plus, Gabrielle made me."

Okay, enough was enough. "Why do you do that?" Preston squared off with his brother, crossing his arms over his chest. "Why can't you just say 'hi' or 'you're welcome'?" Jackson had no idea—or maybe just didn't care—how hard it was for Preston to even thank him in the first place. How impossible it was to have humility in front of someone who probably couldn't find the word in the dictionary.

Someone who already had everything Preston was trying to achieve.

Jackson laughed, stepping out of the way of a passing crew member carrying a ladder. "You're too serious."

"Maybe you're not serious enough."

"I'm here, aren't I?" Jackson waved his clipboard.

Preston exhaled a big breath. "Yes. You are." He tried to remember what Lulu's big smile would look like. It would all be worth it.

"Great." Jackson's expression sobered slightly. "Besides, I wanted to express my condolences in person."

Preston jerked his gaze to his brother. "Condolences?"

"About you and Lulu breaking up." Then his

brother dramatically slapped his hand to his forehead. "Oh, that's right! It's not really a breakup when you never were together, is it?" His grin returned as Preston's frown deepened.

He knew this was coming...had prepared for it. Even prayed about it. Yet still, the sting wedged deep, coated by a layer of humiliation. He breathed another prayer for grace. He'd messed up in creating this whole faux relationship with Lulu, and honestly, he deserved the teasing. At least he felt able to pray again, felt a clear conscience driving him toward the things of the Lord. That was worth the mild persecution from his brother.

But he still had his limits.

Preston took a deep breath. "Go ahead, get it all out of your system while you can. But I'm not going to put up with it for long."

"Yeah, right. What are you going to do?" Jackson smirked, tapping the clipboard against his leg.

"Not fight you, if that's what you're suggesting." Preston lowered his voice and stepped back, away from the traffic of the front door. "What happened, man? We used to be friends."

"Isn't it obvious?" All pretenses gone, Jackson spread his arms wide.

"Not from here," he said.

"Let's just say your shadow runs long."

"What are you talking about?" Preston tugged his brother's sleeve and led him away from the front door, toward the driveway. The sound of hammering and drills provided a measure of privacy for the conversation that was years overdue. "Just spit it out."

"You try growing up as your little brother." Jackson avoided eye contact, running his hand over his shorter hair much the same way Preston always did. "Then we can talk."

Preston crossed his arms over his chest. "Are you *kidding* me? You have everything. A thriving business, a beautiful wife."

Jackson snorted. "Yeah—*your* ex-girlfriend."

Ugh. There he went again. He pointed at his brother. "See? That's my beef. You always have to rub things in my face."

"That wasn't a slam, bro. Don't you see?" Jackson threw out one arm. "One more shadow. One more pair of shoes to fill. You set the bar for everything—Mom and Dad. Grades. Driving. Dating. Even Gabrielle, specifically. I was always a step behind you."

Preston stared at his brother in disbelief. "Well, you're certainly ahead right now."

"And do you know how hard I have to work to stay there? All I heard growing up was 'Preston's so smart. Preston got straight As, Jackson, why do you have a C?'" He shook his head.

"And now it's just 'Preston has such a way with his students' and 'Preston is so mature and capable.'" Jackson glared. "It's a lot to live up to."

"Well, all I hear is how successful you are and why can't I be more like *you*." Preston glowered back.

"Huh." Jackson looked down at the ground, the fight draining from his expression.

He felt the slow release of his own frustration and let out a shaky laugh. "This is something." To put it mildly. Who would have thought? Jackson…jealous of *him*?

His brother sheepishly rubbed the back of his neck. "Yeah, maybe we should stop listening to Mom and Dad, and you know—talk to each other."

"I think you're right." Preston hesitantly held out his hand. After all, it *was* the season for second chances and forgiveness. He knew he needed a lot of it for himself. Why not start with extending it to his only sibling? He swallowed hard. "Truce?"

Jackson evaluated him for a moment, then nodded as he tucked the clipboard under his arm. "Truce." He heartily shook Preston's hand, then pulled him in a step closer. "Now I just have one more question."

"What?" he asked warily.

"How are you going to win Lulu back?"

* * *

"Does it hurt?"

"Of course it hurts, silly. She's got crutches, doesn't she?"

"There's such a thing as pain meds."

"We don't know that she's taken any."

Lulu didn't have to turn around to recognize Tori's, Hayley's and Claudia's voices arguing softly behind her as she lay awkwardly on her side on the floor with a screwdriver. She hid a smile as she continued screwing the outlet cover on the wall, which was still faintly sticky with fresh paint.

"Who comes back to a construction site after a trip to the ER?" Aiden's hushed question, quieter than the girls' comments, still carried clearly across the newly floored space.

"Wonder Woman." Tori's voice dripped with awe.

Lulu rolled over, propped up on one elbow and pointed the screwdriver at them. "You guys, I twisted my ankle. I'm not deaf."

"I heard a crunch," Claudia protested as she squatted on the floor by Lulu. "When you fell out of your car, there was a definite crunch."

"That was the screen of my phone." Lulu finished securing the outlet cover to the wall, then eased up on her good foot. "Can you hand me my crutches?"

Aiden quickly grabbed them from where Lulu had leaned them against the living room doorframe, and Claudia steadied her with a light grip on her shoulder as Lulu hobbled fully to her feet. "Thanks, guys."

Hayley brushed her long hair off her shoulders. "Why did you come back? I'd be home in bed if I had a broken ankle. With ice cream."

"It's not broken." Lulu handed Hayley the screwdriver so she could better grip her crutch handles. "Besides, we're so close. I'm not missing the finish line." Not after everything they'd gone through to get here—especially in the last four hours. Her ankle throbbed at the memory.

Tori's eyes grew wide. "Is it true Claudia drove your car?"

"Don't tell anyone that." Lulu winced. "It was an emergency."

After she'd fallen, she genuinely wondered if her ankle had fractured like her phone screen. Claudia, who had her learner's permit but not a license yet, had eagerly volunteered to drive Lulu the five miles to the Tulip Mound ER, and Lulu had been in no position to argue.

An X-ray, a tightly wrapped bandage and a few ibuprofen later, she'd driven them both back to the Haven Project. Jackson's crew was still at work and had apparently accomplished a Christmas miracle while she'd been away. The cabinets were placed. The floors completed. The sink installed. All the walls had been primed, and several of them, like the living room, had already been painted. The jumpsuit-clad workers had left for the evening but would be back to finish painting the next morning, according to Jackson and his steel clipboard.

They were going to make it.

Jackson strode through the living room then, exhaustion creasing his forehead. "We're about to lock this place up for the night. You guys ready to head out?" It wasn't a suggestion.

"We are. Thanks for doing this." Lulu reached to pat his arm but remembered her crutches just in time and managed to stay upright.

"Don't thank me." Jackson shrugged a little as he looked down to attach his pen back to his clipboard. "Thank my brother."

Lulu's grip tightened on her crutch handles and her breath caught. "Preston?"

"Yeah, your...*boyfriend*?" Jackson smirked a little, his eyes darting back and forth between her and the teenagers surrounding her. "Heard of him?"

"He's not my—I mean, of course." Lulu glanced at Claudia and Hayley, who stared at her suspiciously, and let out a nervous laugh. His parents knew the truth, but she wasn't sure if Jackson did. And the kids definitely didn't—how in the world could she tell them? She hadn't even thought of that. This one lie never seemed to end.

But first... Was she understanding Jackson correctly? "You're saying Preston did this?"

"Wait. You didn't know?" Tori frowned at her. "Why wouldn't he have told you?"

He probably had. With the unread text messages permanently hidden inside her smashed phone. Lulu bit back a groan. Worse yet, Preston probably thought she was ignoring him, even after his grand gesture. Of course, she could ask Jackson to borrow his cell, but she'd have no privacy. Plus the man was practically ushering them to the front door.

"Preston arranged everything so the house would be ready by Christmas Eve. He's the hero here." Jackson made a circular motion in the air with his finger. "Now, everyone out. You can come back in the morning and help paint if you'd like."

Chagrined, Lulu hobbled ahead, flanked by Claudia and Hayley. Aiden held the front door wide for her, casting a nervous glance over his shoulder back into the house as Jackson disappeared toward the kitchen. "Hey, I forgot something in the bathroom. I'll catch y'all later." He hurried back inside before anyone could respond.

"That was weird." Hayley frowned after him as she held the door for Tori.

Claudia walked backward down the short pathway to the driveway. "Not as weird as that whole thing about Teach back there." She shot Lulu a pointed glance.

"He must have wanted to surprise me." Lulu kept strolling past her, down the front walk on her crutches, until she paused to risk a glance back.

All three girls stood staring at her with their arms crossed, as moonlight cast a glow on their hair.

She released a sigh and turned around to face them. "Okay, fine. Busted."

"You broke up?" Confusion filled Tori's eyes.

Claudia palmed her forehead. "No! You were perfect for each other."

"We were actually never really dating. We were…" Lulu blew out her breath. "Pretending. It's a long story."

The girls stared.

She ducked her head. "I'm sorry I lied to you. I could tell you why, but there's really no excuse and I'm tired of making one."

Hayley was the first to break the silence. "That's absurd."

"Yeah, you're adults. Why lie about something like dating?" Claudia frowned.

"No, I meant it was absurd because she and Mr. Green really like each other." Hayley shot Claudia a knowing look. "Obviously."

"We did see them kiss." Tori grinned. "That was real."

"You guys!" Lulu exclaimed as her neck flushed with heat.

"Don't worry, I pulled her away from the window." Claudia nudged Tori in the side with her elbow. "But I agree. That *was* a real kiss."

Lulu didn't need to be reminded. She could still feel Preston's hands in her hair if she stopped long enough—which was precisely why she hadn't. "There's more to the story. I don't think it's that simple this time."

"But he did this for you, didn't he? That's what the new contractor was saying." Tori rolled in her lower lip as she gestured toward the house. "I think you should give him a chance."

She'd love to—but just because Preston called his brother and did the right thing didn't mean he was ready to give her…give *them*…a chance. And she hated to even hope. Besides, she could never do a long-distance relationship. "It's complicated, you guys, but the bottom line is that a relationship between the two of us is not happening."

"You've been wrong before," Tori whispered.

Hayley shushed her.

"Wait." Lulu squinted at the younger girl. "What do you mean?"

"About the night of the auction. You were

afraid no one would bid on you and look what all happened. You brought in the most money of the whole night." Tori shuffled her feet a little and shrugged. "I think sometimes you let your insecurity tell you lies."

The sweet girl's honest words pierced Lulu's heart. "You do?"

"We all do sometimes. And I hate to tell you to take advice from Hayley, but in this case, you should take advice from Hayley." Claudia shoved her hands in her baggy jean pockets as she turned to Lulu. "You're pretty awesome. I would imagine Teach knows that, too."

Tears burned Lulu's eyes. "You guys." She sniffed. "So you're not mad at me for lying?"

"Adults mess up sometimes, too." Claudia shrugged. "It's cool. Just you know—don't do it again."

"And give us more free donuts." Tori grinned.

They were too good to her. The abundance of grace washed over Lulu until she felt she might burst. "Come here." Holding her crutches wide, she opened her arms and balanced like a flamingo until they scooted into her group hug.

"Ugh. I totally just put on fresh mascara," Hayley groaned as she pressed against Lulu's shoulder. "I didn't know we were going to be having a moment."

"Who puts on fresh makeup to go to a construction site?" Claudia pulled back to ask.

"Can we just have the moment, people?" Tori asked from the middle of the hug.

As the girls continued to affectionately bicker, Lulu let the truth of their young wisdom fill her heart. They were right. She'd spent way too much time letting fear of other people's opinions dictate her confidence. Neal's family might have done a number on her heart, but they didn't get the final say. She was better than that.

She was *more* than that.

And there were plenty of people who could see it and remind her. She hugged the girls tightly, despite Hayley's attempt to wriggle out of the circle, and prayed a prayer of gratitude for the timely reminder of forgiveness and acceptance. Maybe she couldn't long-distance date, and maybe Preston would never even ask her to. But it didn't matter. None of that determined her worth or what she brought to the table.

She was Goldilocks...just right to the people in her life who mattered, and more than that, to the God Who saved her. Who continued offering forgiveness and acceptance despite all her imperfections.

It was going to be a great Christmas.

Chapter Nineteen

The festive, garland-and-ribbon-trimmed atmosphere on Main Street Christmas Eve night triggered Preston's hope, but he wouldn't feel better until he could talk to Lulu.

A choir of kids singing "Joy to the World" pulsed through the staticky speakers set around the makeshift gazebo stage. The children were cute, but no amount of holly, Christmas music or hot chocolate would fix what was wrong in his heart.

The problem was, he wasn't sure Lulu was going to give him a chance to make things right.

He stretched up on his toes and continued his search of the crowd for her. She still hadn't answered his texts from yesterday, though Jackson had made a comment late last night about seeing her at the Haven Project. The fact that Lulu knew about the home being completed and still hadn't contacted him sent a message, loud and clear. He'd stopped by Oopsy Daisy and found it closed earlier that afternoon, and quickly talked himself out of dropping by her house uninvited on Christmas Eve. He didn't want her to feel cornered if she was truly avoiding him.

But oh how he hoped she wasn't.

He scanned the crowd, but still didn't spot her anywhere. His parents hovered nearby at the apple cider stand, and his mom lifted one gloved hand in a wave before turning to adjust his dad's scarf. His dad swatted her hand away, then leaned down and pecked her on the cheek.

Preston smiled as he moved along toward the stage. He'd updated his parents that morning about his and Jackson's truce, and his mom had declared it the best Christmas gift she could have asked for. Gabrielle had driven in to be with them for Christmas, now that Jackson was staying through the holiday, and they were currently strolling arm in arm through the crowd. One good thing that had come from all this—he could see his brother smiling with his wife and feel nothing but happiness for him.

"Candle?" Tori and Claudia appeared in front of him, holding a large basket full of miniature candles featuring bulbs instead of wicks. "It's for the choir performance coming up."

"Sure." He picked one from the basket, flicking the candle's off-and-on switch.

"Safety first." Claudia rolled her eyes. "No flames, no fun."

"It's *responsible*," Tori corrected her.

Chuckling despite himself, Preston clicked his candle to off mode and slid it into his jacket pocket. His fingers brushed the gift box he hoped to give Lulu tonight, and he took a deep breath. "Hey, you girls haven't seen Lulu around by chance, have you?"

They shook their heads in unison.

The girls took off before he could say another word. *Strange.* He shook his head as he turned back toward the stage. A glimpse of yellow moving slowly through the choir of kids caught his eye, and he pressed toward the gazebo, following it.

The crowd parted as Lulu emerged above them on the gazebo stage, her yellow scarf draped loosely around her shoulders...and a pair of crutches tucked under her arms.

He stared. When had she hurt herself? And why hadn't Jackson said anything? Was that why she hadn't responded to his texts? His thoughts raced, trying to connect dots he didn't fully have.

If the injury was very recent, she didn't appear to be in pain. She looked fine. No, *beautiful*, in that bright scarf that lit her eyes and complexion. She seemed downright giddy even, as she awkwardly reached around her crutches to adjust the microphone height.

"Good evening!" Feedback squealed, and Lulu ducked as half the crowd groaned and covered their ears. Someone wearing black and standing near the speakers made an adjustment, and the noise abruptly ceased.

"Sorry about that." She laughed breathlessly into the microphone, and Preston stood transfixed by the confidence radiating on her face.

A little bit of time away from him had clearly done her good.

He swallowed hard, unable to look away as Lulu pulled an envelope from the pocket of her coat.

"I was honored to be asked by the Haven Project to read the winner of tonight's Home for the Holidays giveaway. I'm sure you're all familiar with the project on Fern Avenue that's been going on for several months now, and well… This is it!" She waved the envelope at her audience. "The big moment is here. Someone is about to get a house!"

The crowd hummed with excitement, voices mingling together in appreciative tones. He cast a glance around the now-familiar faces, surprised to realize he recognized more people than he expected.

Principal Crowder stood nearby with her family, wearing an oversize floppy hat that looked handmade. Probably a gift from one of the students at the high school. Noah Montgomery from the inn was there, too, holding a cup of hot chocolate. And Tori stood near her uncle, grinning at Lulu, while Claudia hovered next to her, attempting to braid Hayley's hair as Hayley kept slapping her hands away. Aiden was with them, as well, his hands shoved in the pockets of the jacket Preston had given him as he stood a few steps back from the girls. A peaceful recognition washed over Preston, one he hadn't felt in years.

Home. Tulip Mound was becoming home.

"Open it already!" a little kid suddenly shouted from the back.

Everyone laughed. But instead of blushing as he'd expected, Lulu simply beamed. "I will! But first, I need to say something." She adjusted the microphone again, and one of her crutches wobbled precariously. She caught it just in time before it fell off the stage. "Oops. That's sort of how I got this injury in the first place." She kicked out her bandage-wrapped foot, and the crowd laughed.

A flood of emotion crowded Preston's heart as he joined the lighthearted clapping around him. He'd never been so proud of Lulu. Something had clearly shifted for her over the last few days, but the fact that he'd missed it because of his own selfishness cut him to the core.

He just hoped he wasn't too late.

"As some of you regular volunteers know, this house almost didn't happen in time." Lulu paused. "There were multiple setbacks and then when the crew got relocated for emergency storm repair last-minute, I started to panic. I hated the thought of this house not being ready by tonight." She shifted her weight on her crutches, the envelope clutched in one hand. "However, a really smart man I know told me that it would get done, and it would be okay if it happened a week or two after Christmas."

Preston's chest tightened. Where was she going with this? She didn't sound mad. But still…

"And he would have been right. But this really smart man also made sure another crew came in and got the job done on time—all at a personal sacrifice to himself." She caught Preston's eye then and smiled, and his breath caught. She wasn't mad.

He still had a chance.

Hope swelled until he thought he would burst.

"And a very special thanks to Jackson Green and his workers for making the impossible possible." Lulu turned and nodded at someone in the crowd. Preston followed her gaze to Jackson, who toasted her with a cup of cocoa.

"What this really smart man didn't realize was *why* it was so important to me that the Home for the Holidays be completed on time, and why I hated the thought of the winning family being asked to wait to move into their new home." She took a breath, the deep inhale evident through the microphone. Then her gaze locked on Preston's. "Because that family, once upon a time, was my own."

He held her gaze, keeping his face stoic for her sake, even as he internally felt himself collapse. Lulu had been in that kind of position before? He couldn't even picture that.

"I grew up with a single parent, and we didn't have much. My mom did an amazing job with me, and we made it through. She volunteers regularly now for the Haven Project, too, and is currently overseas building a house for a family in need. I'm proud of her." Lulu's voice hitched with emotion.

Hurt for her past gnawed at Preston's stomach. He couldn't stand the thought of a child version of Lulu not having everything she needed. No wonder she'd gotten so upset when he hadn't initially taken the opportunity to call Jackson. The final puzzle pieces slid into place.

He wished she'd have trusted him enough to tell him the whole story before now. But after the way he'd acted, practically shoving his mother's ring at her during that argument over the house, well… He didn't blame her.

And yet it seemed like she'd forgiven him, despite the lack of text responses. He'd never been so grateful, and never felt so undeserving.

"I used to be embarrassed about this part of my past, but now, I realize there's nothing to be ashamed of. Because at the end of the day, we're all in need. In need of love and compassion, and understanding. In need of forgiveness." Lulu's chin quivered a little then, and Preston fought back his own press of tears as he held her in his gaze. "And in need of a Savior. Not just at Christmas, but all year round."

A reverent silence filled the outdoor space, only the low hum of the speakers evident as everyone processed the moment. She was right. Preston didn't have to be perfect, or strive to be the best, or even be deserving, because no one was. He'd messed up and lied. Been selfish. He'd hurt the people he loved most in the world.

But because of the baby who came to a manger one special night, there was hope. Tonight, and every night.

Someone quietly clicked on their candle, and soon, one by one, tiny beacons of light broke the darkness. Then Charlie, Tori's aunt, began singing "Silent Night" in a lovely soprano. The candles began to sway, until everyone joined in with the spontaneous Christmas hymn.

On the stage, Lulu pressed her fingers to her lips, a smile sneaking behind her hand as tears streamed down her face. The song ended, and she whispered into the microphone. "Thank you. That was beautiful."

"We love you, Lulu!" Claudia called out from the crowd. Tori and Hayley voiced their hearty agreement, then someone in the back shouted, "All hail the donut queen!"

A few people laughed, Lulu blushed and Noah Montgomery repeated the chant. Principal Crowder joined in, then all the teenagers.

"You guys." Choked up, Lulu waved the hand still holding the envelope. "I appreciate you all so much. But enough about me. Tonight is about someone else."

"Drumroll!" someone shouted.

A sudden round of patted knees and clapping hands created a plethora of chaotic noise. "Close enough." Lulu laughed as she ripped open the envelope and removed a note card and a house key. "And the winning family is… Heather Raines! And her son…" Her eyes widened as she read further. "…Aiden Raines."

Handing the keys to Aiden's mom and holding back the happy sob threatening to break free had been one of the hardest things Lulu had ever done. But she hadn't wanted to embarrass them—especially Aiden—and had tried to keep her emotions in check as she connected his mother with the Haven Project director, who would walk them through all they needed to know about taking ownership of their new home.

From an out-of-the-way corner of the grounds near the parking lot, Lulu gripped her crutches and watched Aiden now with his mother near the gazebo, sipping hot chocolate with the Haven Project director, their faces alight with joy and lingering shock. She knew the feeling—those exact emotions still welled in her own chest.

She couldn't believe she hadn't noticed how bad things had gotten with Aiden and hadn't known the bank foreclosed on their home six months ago. Sure, he'd been sneaking around the jobsite, but she had no idea he'd slept there a few nights after the crew had gone home, so he wouldn't have to sleep in his mom's van alone while she worked a double shift at the truck stop diner outside Tulip Mound. Had no idea he'd been showering at school in the locker room early before class.

All the details that had come pouring out of him as he held the key to his new house.

"Hey."

Lulu spun toward the voice behind her, losing her grip on her crutches. She hopped once to steady herself, but then Preston's strong hands supported her, and she caught her balance.

"Hi." She looked up at him.

His smile was cautious, but genuine. She didn't blame him. Who knew what he must think about her prolonged silence. There was so much to explain, she wasn't sure where to start. "My, uh, phone broke." She adjusted her grip on her crutches. "Because I sort of landed on it."

"I can see that." He nodded toward her ankle. "Are you okay?"

"Just a bad bruise. I should be fine to walk in a few days." She rolled in her lower lip as she looked up at him. She had to know… "Do your parents hate me?"

"Of course not. Quite the opposite." Preston shook his head. "They understand why we did it and accepted both our apologies. We had a big talk. I actually texted you about all of that and passed on some messages from them. Dad was worried about you, especially."

"I'm sorry I never got to read them—or your texts about the Haven Project." She sighed. "And on that note, I'm also sorry I was so pushy about your brother."

He took a step closer toward her as the children's choir began singing a rousing rendition of "Jingle Bells" from the stage. "Don't be. I needed that."

She felt like she sort of needed him.

But she pressed her lips together and nodded, unable to read the expression on his face. Was he disappointed? Had he taken her public confession well, or was that pity lingering behind his half smile?

She might as well get everything out now. "Apparently I had a secret of my own all this time."

"I'm starting to realize those aren't usually a good idea." Preston let out a chuckle, one she still couldn't fully decipher. Then his expression grew serious. "Lulu, why didn't you tell me? Then I would have understood why this project was so important to you."

"I was afraid that was all you'd see when you looked at me—the girl with the too-small coat, and one pair of pinched shoes. The girl who knows what it's like to live in a car for a season." Lulu shrugged, avoiding his attentive gaze. That was all Neal and his family had seen. But Preston kept proving himself differently, didn't he?

The last few days had felt like a waltz of a few steps forward and uncounted steps back, but she *was* learning about accepting herself for who she was—and all the things in her life that had shaped her into that person. Her public confession was just the first step of many.

She didn't want to be afraid anymore.

Preston reached into his jacket and removed a gift-wrapped box. "Do you want to know what I see when I look at you?" He pressed the gift into her hands. "Open that."

She tugged the red bow off the small gold box, looked around, then awkwardly tried to shove the ribbon into her pocket. Her crutches wobbled.

Preston laughed and took the bow from her. "Allow me."

She lifted the lid and removed a dainty rose gold bracelet. She gingerly touched each of the little charms, smiling. A bicycle. A donut. A hammer.

And a piece of mistletoe.

She swallowed, avoiding his eyes.

Preston reached out and gently laid both hands on her shoulders. "That's what I see when I look at you."

"A bicycle and a hammer?" She let out a muffled half laugh, half snort. Afraid to hope. Afraid to be fully seen. She'd come so far, but this kind of vulnerability felt like a boot camp for her newfound confidence.

Preston gingerly lifted her chin to meet his gaze. "I see a woman who started a thriving business and provides not only the best donuts I've ever eaten, but a safe spot for teenagers to land." He quickly continued. "And before you argue about the donuts, it's only *one* element of what you do. It's not your sum."

She rubbed her finger against the sprinkled donut on the bracelet. "I think I'm starting to realize the same." It was a part of her...a part she was proud of...but not the totality of what she had to offer.

Preston grinned. "But you really are the donut queen. I'd wear that crown proudly if I were you." Then he touched the hammer charm on the bracelet. "I also see a woman with a passion for others. A passion so strong, in fact, that she donates time and money, even with a sprained ankle, to make sure people have what they need."

She winced. "And insults her friends along the way."

"Well, like I said, I'm pretty sure that *friend* needed the wake-up call." He touched the next charm. "A bicycle, because...that was the site of one of our first outings."

"Ironic. I signed up for spin class to avoid dating."

Confusion furrowed his brow.

"Never mind."

He shrugged. "I just remember how cute you

were, trying to play off the fact that you'd fallen off your bike right when I walked up."

"Your timing *was* pretty horrible."

Preston's expression sobered. "I think I was right on time, actually. That was one of the first moments I really saw you."

"Right—on the ground. Sweaty from spin class with my hair plastered to my face." Lulu grimaced.

"Sure, you were on the ground, and sweaty. But you jumped up. Asked me why I wasn't at church. And then took me to the Haven Project site." He gazed deep into her eyes. "I think that was when I realized I'd probably have followed you anywhere."

Her heart skipped, then thundered to catch up. This wasn't a man pitying her. Or judging her. Or doing anything other than romancing her holiday-themed socks off.

But just because they'd been able to forgive each other and move forward didn't change the looming cloud hovering over their future.

"Preston…" She reluctantly pressed her hand against his chest, gently urging him back a few inches. "That might be true, but you're leaving. You can't follow me if I'm not going to Colorado."

"I know. That's all I thought about the last few days." Preston closed his hand over hers, still resting on the center of his shirt. "I was going to ask you to consider long-distance dating. Or at least date me until the summer, so we could give this thing between us a real try."

Uncertainty struck her heart. *"Was?"*

"I changed my mind."

Her heart stammered, and she tried to tug her hand free. She should have known better. "I understand."

"I don't think you do." He pulled her closer, his hand still covering hers. "I'm not going to Colorado. Or anywhere."

She stiffened. "You're not?"

"Seeing you on stage tonight, being in that crowd, surrounded by all the teens and watching Aiden win the house..." He shook his head. "There's nothing like it. Tulip Mound is my home, Lulu. I don't need a prestigious position to give me anything more than I already have right here." He dipped his head until his gaze caught hers. "With you."

Her stomach flipped. Preston should have been an English major instead of history—he was right up there with the poets. Keats and Browning had nothing on this man. But this sounded too good to be true. Pretending with Preston had been easy.

Being real was scary.

Lulu drew a shaky breath. "What if you

change your mind, or resent me for losing the opportunity?" She'd rather things between them end now than that happen.

"It's not just about you. I can't bail on these kids, either." Preston shrugged a little. "I want to be here for Aiden, and all the others. Want to volunteer for their next auction and help build the next project house."

"We do always need volunteers." She realized she was out of excuses to doubt and full of several good reasons to hope. Her heart felt like it was trying to climb out of her chest and leap straight into his hands. It was quickly becoming his.

As it had been for weeks.

She drew a shaky breath as she balanced with her crutches. "So what are you saying, exactly?"

Preston gazed down at her. "I'm saying... I want to keep buying you charms, Lulu Boyd. Because I'm falling for you, if you haven't noticed that yet."

"Well, I'm fairly certain the sentiment is mutual."

He cradled her face, his thumb grazing her jaw. "And I'm also saying that final charm might be my favorite."

"Ah... So you're saying when you look at me, you see a clump of plants?"

Undeterred, he moved closer, his fingers sliding into her hair. "More like, I remember one particular plant that I happen to be very fond of."

"I think it's my favorite, too." Her voice escaped in a whisper as he closed the distance between them, inch by inch.

His thumb glided down her cheek, leaving a trail of warmth. "More so than daisies?"

Her eyes closed to half-mast as her crutches fell to the ground. She didn't care. She hung on to him instead. "I think I just forgot what daisies looked like."

"Mistletoe looks pretty good at the moment."

"Agreed."

He was close now, so close she could detect the aroma of peppermint hot chocolate mixing with that musky forest cologne she'd always loved so much. The festive din happening across the grounds faded until it was just the two of them, gazing at each other. Offering second chances under the mistletoe.

The fact that there wasn't any mistletoe this time was not an important factor.

Lulu fully closed her eyes, and the next thing she knew, his lips covered hers, a kiss full of promise and potential and joyful hope.

Christmas had come early.

Epilogue

One Year Later

Strains of "O Holy Night" drifted up the aisle of the church toward the cracked door where Lulu anxiously waited. She adjusted the skirt of her white gown and drew a steadying breath as a very pregnant Gabrielle waddled down the rose-petal-covered carpet toward the candlelit stage.

It was almost time.

"You look beautiful." Harold smiled down at Lulu, patting her hand that was tucked through the crook of his arm as they awaited their cue. "Don't worry."

"I was actually more worried about tripping, but thank you." Lulu's hands were growing sweaty, but Preston liked her quirks. Right?

"My boy is crazy in love with you—quit worrying about that, too. I'm getting to where I can read your eyes, you know." Then Harold pulled a handkerchief from his tuxedo jacket pocket. "And here." He shot her a knowing wink.

Lulu laughed, hugging his arm as she took the white cloth and wiped her palms. "I'm glad you're here."

"Me, too, darling."

After several rounds of treatment, Harold was officially back in remission and had been for some time. So far, all his checkups continued to prove he was the picture of health—which he loved to remind Susie about when she started hovering a little too close. Thankfully, with Jackson and Gabrielle's baby due right after the new year, she'd have a new outlet for her attention.

The music shifted to the "Bridal Chorus," and all the nerves in Lulu's stomach gathered into a bunch and then nosedived toward her feet—which were currently covered in white satin ballet slippers. Lulu tightened her grip on Harold's arm as the ushers opened the church door, the weight of the family heirloom ring residing on her finger reminding her she was chosen. She was too much and not enough and all of that was okay.

She was Preston's Goldilocks, and that was just right.

The music swelled, and the next thing she knew, she was gliding down the aisle, Harold's hand patting hers reassuringly as they passed pews full of Lulu's favorite people, including half the teens from the high school. Her mother, recently back from another overseas building mission, blew her a kiss from her seat in the front row next to Susie, who smiled with teary eyes.

Then Lulu's gaze locked on Preston's, waiting for her at the end of the petal-strewn aisle and looking more handsome than ever in his tux. Sudden peace filled her heart, replacing the nerves and her fear of tripping.

She smiled at him—her groom. "Merry Christmas," she mouthed at him as the minister began to address the congregation.

"Merry Christmas," he mouthed back, his eyes drinking her in as if she was a precious gift.

As they joined hands and turned to face the minister, Lulu did trip over her long train. And Preston caught her, like he specifically promised in their vows to do every day for the rest of his life.

All her Christmases just kept getting merrier.

* * * * *

Dear Reader,

Secrets can be tricky, can't they? There is such a fine line between secrets and lies...and even lies and surprises. After all, we often lie in order to pull off a surprise party or a Christmas gift for a loved one. Culturally, we view those lies as acceptable. It can still be stressful, though!

One of the harder secrets I've ever carried was about five years ago, when my husband and I decided to buy a new house and not tell a soul. This was the first house we bought together after starting our blended family (after walking through unwanted divorces) and we wanted to surprise our children. After months of secret meetings and whispered conversations and close calls, we pulled it off, but it was exhausting!

Surprising a loved one with a gift can be fun, but most of the time, lies and secrets get us into trouble—even when we think we have a good reason. Lulu and Preston had to figure that out the hard way, and for a time, everything blew up in their faces as a result.

As cliché as it sounds, honesty is always the best policy. I hope journeying with Lulu and Preston through their tangled web of good intentions makes you laugh, but also reminds you of the beauty found in genuine communication and integrity.

Be blessed!
Betsy St. Amant

Get 3 FREE REWARDS!

We'll send you 2 FREE Books plus a FREE Mystery Gift.

FREE
Value Over
$20

Both the **Love Inspired®** and **Love Inspired® Suspense** series feature compelling novels filled with inspirational romance, faith, forgiveness and hope.

Get 3 FREE REWARDS!

We'll send you 2 FREE Books plus a FREE Mystery Gift.

FREE Value Over $20

Both the **Harlequin® Special Edition** and **Harlequin® Heartwarming™** series feature compelling novels filled with stories of love and strength where the bonds of friendship, family and community unite.